EYES
An Anthology of Horror Stories

I0683047

Edited by Dorothy Davies

EYES
An Anthology of Horror Stories

GRAVESTONE PRESS

CONTENTS

CONTENTS

Where The Crow Flies

Wendy Lynn Newton

"They say a bird flew out of Tamsey Abbott's eye when she was born.

"Black, with wings tipped in emerald and indigo and beady golden eyes that landed square on the midwife's own before it flew through the attic window and made its way towards Abbott's Woods, with not so much as a *caw* for explanation as her mother drew her last breath.

"Not a small bird like the fledglings that circle Ol' Tomsons' barn each August, they claim, when the crabapples turn red as the leaves and wrinkle to mush as they ready to fall. It was as big as Papa Abbott's fist after he'd sunk a jug of Brownie's malt and as black as the mark on Mama Abbott's arm Betsie swore she saw that day, as she watched her peg the laundry under the hayloft and her pinafore sleeve rose high enough to make Betsie flush and turn away.

"Never been right," Brownie says, taking a drag on a yellowed corn-cob pipe. The cramped room sweetens with the smell of peat and smoke from an autumn bonfire and he throws another faggot onto the flames. Not much is heard in the space between as they wait for Brownie's story, heard a hundred times before in this same inn, on nights as dark and cold as this one. There's only the crackle and pop of the pinewood and the rush of the orange flames

7

as they lick the fireplace and dance over the grate and a single intake of air as the townspeople hold their breath to listen.

"When she grewed, that eye never opened far enough to see the world outside," he starts again. "Can't blame 'er for that," and there's a few nods and whispers of, "Aye, he's right on that one."

"She wore the black mark of that crow, bone-deep as her Mama did, only her poor bird never escaped. Some say it grew in her belly until the day she birthed Tamsey and it was passed on from mother to daughter as real as her blood and as sharp as her pain. And if you looked into that young girl's eye - "

Several faces lean in towards Brownie.

"If you dared to - "

There is a clinking of glasses as someone jostles the broad oak table and a circular "Shhhhh," rises gently in unison.

"Well, some say you could see nothing but the black footprint of that bird and a queer expression on Tamsey's face like she was waiting for it to come home to roost."

"Never let go of nothin', those ones," Joe Healy adds as he drags on the sweet-spiced, bitter-hopped beer. "You see 'em hoarding things high in them nests, trophies like. Was bound to come back one day to claim what was his. They never forget."

"They say a bird like that doesn't wait too long to come back," Brownie adds and William Buckley nudges Joe to stop him interrupting again. "It bides its time; waiting for the right moment when it can

8

steal what it claims is his. Who could tell when that would be?"

"I hear'd Frankie Gordon seen it once," Joe says, ignoring William's glare, "right before it happened," and the room takes on a suffocating hush as he picks up the storytelling.

"Most steered clear of Abbott's farm, ol' Papa Abbott, he had a real ripe temper, but Frankie, he needs to get home real sharp one night, get in before his missus cottons on he's messing 'bout with that Millie Dowd. He's cuttin' through the field that lines up right outside Tamsey's room when he looks up and sees the shadow of that bird, black as her eye and huge as a man, framed inside her window. Perched over her like that while she slept."

There's a single cough and a shuffle of feet as everyone's eyes fix on Joe.

"Ol' Frankie, he wants to call out, but he's scared, see, and then he hears it, loud, he says, as loud as the crows that fly each night into Abbott's Woods. Cawing from that upstairs bedroom window, so sad and plaintive it made Frankie's heart ache. As if Tamsey's bird was caught in some great trap set by Papa Abbott's hand."

There is a low murmur as heads bow towards the table, and the fire snaps and spits in the hearth.

"No-one knows for sure when the bird returned, only that it happens and no-one knows why," Brownie continues, "least, why that night, of all nights, I mean."

His pipe lays cold by his hand, but his eye lingers on Joe's. "Some say it was the newly-skinned doe hide Papa Abbott tacked over her

9

bedroom window, pale as her own skin and just as soft. Others claim it was the foot he cut from the lame buck she saved and rammed into the keyhole of her door, so's it couldn't be opened, 'cept from the outside. Couldn't get out, they said, and you should never trap a wild thing. And they'd seen the wild that had flown from her eye on the day she was born. Trapped like that, most said it was nature fighting back."

"Nature does what nature is," mumbled William and Brownie raises his glass as if to toast.

"When they found him like that in her room, with his eyes clawed from his skull and the flesh of his hands pecked to shreds, they knew'd what had happened. Even before they seen that long, black feather quill tipped with emerald and indigo jammed into his heart."

"The crow had come home to roost," Joe mutters and Brownie nods, a queer half-smile on his face.

"Some swear they saw it, her bird, flying from her bedroom window that day, on wings as black as ash from one of Cutter's spring bonfires, graceful as an angel's as it flew into Abbott's woods. Others swear they heard it, clear as a church bell, a sweet *caw caw caw* as it swooped overhead. Sheriff Brody frowned through the whole inquest, but even he had no choice. *Natural causes,* he confirmed, for it was nature for sure that had killed him. And they buried Papa Abbott under a pile of white stones in a sad, forgotten place far away from where Tamsey's mother lay."

10

A curl of smoke drifts up to the rafters as Brownie pauses and takes a sip of beer.

"I hear'd she goes looking for that bird."

And Brownie turns a dark eye to Joe and nods.

"At night, they say, when the north wind whispers through the trees and the leaves shake, when the white doe-tails flit through the woods like snow-capped fireflies and even the brown-flecked bucks are safe down in their burrows, you can hear her *caw* as loud and woeful as the ravens that line Ol' Thomson's fence at dusk."

"Frankie reckons it's the same sound he hear'd that night, coming from Tamsey's open window," Joe adds and Brownie's eyes turn sad.

"When the moon is ripe and her blood is set to stir, she takes flight with feet bare to the mud, cracking open the old, oak gate at the end of the loke and heads straight to Abbott's woods where the crows nest, high at the peak of the giant oaks where the moonlight is at its fullest. There she flies, leaving behind an attic bedroom fixed in shadow, till her feet are as light as feathers, and the curve of her back is nothing more than a blur of wings slipping further away into the dark."

When Eyes Don't Close

Olivia Arieti

Neville considered himself a lucky guy; he was a successful businessman and happily married to Alice, his high school sweetheart. The couple, young and charming, lived in an elegant house in the outskirts with a big garden and a swimming pool where they often threw parties especially on summer evenings. Alice's liveliness was amusing him while her lovely silhouette never stopped seducing him. Her eyes, in particular, had always intrigued him, gleaming with enthusiasm and glee during the day, with wanton desire at night time.

When the devoted husband met Jinny, his whole world crumbled and he had to admit that there was a woman more beautiful and appealing than his wife.

It was a total shock, a challenge or rather a menace to his wellbeing and certainties. Doubts entered his mind, lust his heart; Jinny's image followed him everywhere.

'Perhaps, if I talk to her, go as far as having a drink, I would get her off my mind,' thought Neville, confident that it was only a momentary crush. The girl wasn't his type. True, she was gorgeous but had more the aspect of the *femme fatal* that never attracted him. The veiled black stockings that made her legs so seductive, however, flashed before him and he wondered what it would be like to pull them off slowly and catch a glimpse of her lingerie that surely was black as well...

Never had a drink been more fatal. Jinny personified sensuality and let it seep from every pore. Her smile was voluptuous, her voice a continuous invitation, her touch mesmerising. There was nothing he could do about.

On returning home, Neville realised he had to organise his new life. Alice's darling husband and at the same time, Jinny's passionate lover were his new roles.

For a while everything went smoothly, he even felt flattered by how he could handle the situation. Roses were sent profusely and also some expensive gift was made to assure his girls' happiness.

Suddenly, though, what gave him most pleasure and merriment turned into a deep pain, a heavy burden. He felt split in two. Half of his heart, mind, of his whole body belonged to Alice, while the other half to Jinny. The strange feeling scared him. Having to shift from one Neville to the other was depressing, exhausting, just as the lies and excuses he had to make up; also the expenses ended up worrying him and his nights became sleepless. He was on the point of a nervous breakdown.

One night, while in Jinny's cosy bedroom, just before she turned out the light, the usual prelude to their wild encounters, he saw Alice's face in the mirror. Her eyes were twinkling bujt they held a dark secret.

"What's the matter, sweetie?" asked his lover. "You know we don't have much time."

"She's found out," he replied, frightened, "I've got to go," and without further explanation, rushed home.

His wife was sleeping like a child, only her mouth had curled in a derisory expression.

For the first time he felt sorry and kissed her tenderly. Nothing but a stupid hallucination due to his exhaustion.

When the following evening they were having dinner, Jinny's eyes appeared in the dining room mirror.

Wide open, they glared at him as though stating, "I have to talk to you."

"What are you staring at, honey? That mirror has always been there."

"Simply admiring the golden frame, you know I love antiques."

"My granny always said mirrors are sly friends... They show what you don't want to see."

***

Jinny was more gorgeous than ever when he called on her again. Her shameless lust kindled his senses at once; he took her in his arms and kissed her passionately till she pushed him away, fixed her purple eyes on his and said, "Marry me."

Neville was taken aback. She heard no reasons, dragged him in bed and let her wantonness devour him as though it was the last time.

While buttoning up his shirt, he discerned Alice's eyes once again. They were crying.

"She knows," he said, "this time I'm sure."

"It will make things easier," sneered his mistress, "I bet you do want to come back."

The following evening he asked Alice for a divorce. He had just finished talking and Jinny's eyes brightened the mirror to the point that it blurred his sight.

"I love you too much, darling, I'll never give you up, never."

The last word was pronounced slowly, gravely, and it kept resounding in his ears, a dooming toll.

That night was another sleepless one for Neville. He remained in the dining room drinking and staring at the infamous mirror. First he saw Alice's red eyes, then Jinny's scornful ones; they kept shining before him, everywhere, even when he moved over to the pool for some fresh air. Now the vitreous balls were floating on the surface gazing, glaring, sneering at him, spying on his moves. He had to get rid of them!

Like a mad man he jumped into the water and tried to get hold of the scary little spheres that had multiplied and, like bubbles, faded in his hands as soon as he grasped them.

His women's eyes had become a haunt. They would pursue him wherever, each mirror would show them, revealing their feelings whether of sorrow, wrath or pleasure.

Despair seized him on realising Alice would never let him go. She now appeared as a stupid and frivolous creature, an insurmountable obstacle to his true happiness.

There was one way only to obtain his freedom, also from her bloody eyes... He had to close them forever. The horrid thought instantly became a murderous urge, the raptus of a psycho.

He snatched a knife, ran into the bedroom, his clothes still dripping with water and stabbed her.

Neville shuddered before the wide open eyes that kept staring at him both bewildered and menacing, a promise of imminent mayhem, of an unbreakable curse. He could neither continue looking at them nor pull down the lids.

Whatever, she deserved it, her fault if he had become insane, at least half insane; the other part of him luckily, was as lucid as ever. The strange feeling had turned paranoid.

After removing all evidence confident that nobody would ever suspect such a caring husband, he drove over to Jinny's place eager to tell her the good news. Alice had consented to divorce.

As expected, no suspicion fell upon him and after a decent mourning period, he married his mistress.

***

The couple decided to spend the honeymoon abroad, miles away from home.

The many mirrors in their hotel room disturbed Neville, while Jinny smiled, delighted.

"We'll have great fun here, darling," she whispered alluringly and began to undress.

"The trip has tired me, baby, I'll go for a walk along the lake, then I'll be back, all for you," and hurriedly went out before she could say anything.

16

The night was warm and starry, a soft breeze caressed his face as delicate as a woman's touch... Alice's happy face flashed before him and he regretted for letting the situation get out of control.

On gazing at the moonlit surface, however, he distinguished his ex-wife's eyes sneering at him... They hadn't died with her, a truly wicked trick. Simply another hallucination, he assured himself, but shuddered on distinguishing them also in the mirrors of the room, a haunting vision that made him delirious. They were intruding in his privacy, in his soul.

"Go away," he shouted before the stunned Jinny. "Go away!"

"Hey, what's going on, Neville? Who are you yelling at?"

"Can't you scc Alicc's cyes are glaring at me? Killing her hadn't been enough..." an added, "I should have closed those damned eyes immediately, without giving them the chance to launch a curse on me."

The revelation struck his new wife who stood speechless unable to figure out if he was drunk, mad or a true killer.

Furious for letting his heinous deed slip out, he shouted, "Say, you, too, are glaring at me, huh? This time I'll poke them out directly so besides shutting your mouth forever, those deadly balls won't trouble me again."

Before the woman could run out, he got hold of her, took out his jack-knife and did exactly what he said.

Blood flooded all around and the face despite the empty sockets, showed a terrifying diabolic expression. He had to get out of there. He quickly changed, jumped into his car and left.

No eyes to close this time.

The lights blurred the windscreen that continuously showed his wive's eyes, winking one at the other as if conjecturing a dreadful plan...

A few miles after, the car skidded and smashed against a tree.

The madman died on the spot before the ladies' satisfied glances.

Second Jab

Stuart Holland

Grace lay in bed, pondering the day just gone. She had been in two minds about having the second Covid vaccine but a phone call to her parents had convinced her that the risks were so low the benefits far outweighed them. Having had no symptoms from the first jab, she decided to keep the appointment for the second. That had been six hours earlier and, now in bed, there were no symptoms – not yet. The glass of white wine with her evening meal had turned into two. Then, just when she thought everything really was all right, she was suddenly aware of an ache in her upper arm. . For a moment, Grace thought nothing of it. The nurses all said a bit of soreness was a very common side-effect, not to worry, just take paracetamol.

Grace could not be considered a hypochondriac and in her drowsy state, ignored the thoughts of pain relief and slowly drifted off to sleep. Sometime later, deeply unconscious, Grace dreamed strange dreams. Her arm felt like it was on fire, yet she could not wake up. The heat spread down her arm to her wrist and hand, and then up into her neck and her face.

She reached up her other hand to feel her face. Some sticky substance oozed onto her fingers as the dream became more intense. She could smell burning, almost breathe in the fumes and her flesh felt like it was literally burning.

Grace tossed around in her sleep, trying to wake from the nightmare engulfing her, but unable to rouse herself. The burning sensation was spreading into her torso and on down into her legs. It felt in her nightmare, that she was being engulfed by whatever was happening to her. And so it continued, the weird, otherworldly feeling of being consumed by something burning through her. There was respite as the nightmare faded, only for it to return to haunt her even more vividly than before.

Finally Grace opened an eye. It was no longer dark; the first rays of dawn had penetrated her room. Not a full light but a ghostly one that cast eerie shapes across the ceiling, as if a troupe of dancing spirits had gathered. Grace opened the other eye but the apparition did not change. Scared now, she sat bolt up in bed, looking at the floor-length mirror on the wall opposite her. For a moment Grace was confused – she could not see herself in the mirror, yet it was light enough to at least see something. Then confusion turned to panic. She shuffled forward on the bed and looked again – still no reflection. Grace reached forward and made as if to rub the mirror with her hand, as if she thought it might be clouded over. It wasn't.

Grace screamed as she reached forward. Her arm was swollen, covered in dark patches and blood. In blind panic she turned round to see…

… Her body lying peacefully, grey and lifeless, in her bed.

20

A howl of anguish and disbelief filled the room as the spirits above her on the ceiling took on a new reality.

Grace looked through the gloom at them – all covered in blood with darkened, burned flesh, oozing, suppurating something otherworldly.

"They said it was worth the risk," she heard as one voice after another echoed the words.

The Eyes Have It

Rie Sheridan Rose

Some people are drawn to a fine figure. Some like the way another's hair blows in the wind. Some are breast men. Some like ass. For me, it's all about the eyes.

My first memories are of my mother looking down at me with her big, beautiful blue eyes. They fascinated me... those blue irises, the pupils changing size as she looked at me. I wanted them. I reached up to take them—and got my hand swatted for poking her in the eye. She wore glasses from then on. Protecting her treasures. Look but don't touch.

I drew eyes everywhere. Trying to understand them before I had the cognizance to read about them in books. My first specimens in my collection were from insects and roadkill. But the bugs were too tiny to be satisfying and the wheels that bumped over the small animals often crushed the eyes as well. Still, by the time I was five, I had started my life-long hobby.

School was sensory overload until I learned to keep my head down and focus on the work rather than the myriad eyes around me. Blue, brown, green, hazel—so many shades, numerous shapes, a treasure trove of ocular input. I paid close attention in science class and my collection continued to grow.

We lived in a small town with close knit family ties and when I was ten, it was decided I should earn my own pocket money by working for my grandfather in his funeral parlor. It was a distinct pleasure. Here was a chance to study the human eye up close—snatching glimpses before the lids were closed and sometimes prying up those lids when no one was looking to stare into the clouded orbs.

Sometimes, due to accident or nature, an eye would be missing and Grandpa would seat a marble or other small orb into the socket before closing the lid to make the semblance of sleep more natural. This trick was very useful to me. My first human samples were harvested from his parlor and placed in his own formaldehyde with no one the wiser. Well... perhaps *someone* the wiser, because he started locking the doors when he wasn't with me, keeping me away from unattended corpses.

I just learned to be more careful. And to pick locks.

The unfortunate thing about these specimens was that death almost instantly began to cloud the eyes. I had no human eyeballs in my collection that were sharp and vibrant. This was a puzzle I vowed to solve.

By the time I finished high school, I had determined to study ophthalmology. This would give me access to all the eyes I could ever want. Medical school was fascinating and dissecting cadavers my favorite part.

I even loved ER rotation and often switched with fellow classmates who weren't so enamored of it. One night a young gang member came in. He had been shot in the face. We weren't able to save his eye—but it went home with me tucked into its own bottle of formaldehyde hidden in my lunch pail.

I had been experimenting with various resins as a means to preserve a specimen without clouding. The banger's eyeball became my first successful sample. It retained its full color and vibrance. I laid it in its little plastic cube in a place of honor.

By this time I was living alone in a two-bedroom apartment. The second bedroom was my trophy room. The best specimens of my collection were on display there for my eyes alone. I kept the room locked with a key around my neck. No one was allowed inside.

After graduation, I set out my shingle downtown. I soon had a booming practice, as eyes are forever in need of correction lenses. For a while it was enough just to work with eyes all day long, six days a week. My collection held steady. The need to harvest was sublimated by the work.

Then one day, Hannah walked into my office. I stared, too stunned to speak. The walls of my trophy room were plastered with posters and photographs of people with heterochromia iridis, but Hannah was the first living example I had ever seen. One eye was a piercing blue, the other a warm brown. I had to have them.

The silence almost cost me as she became nervous. "Dr. Laughton? I've come to see you because I've been having these headaches..."

I pulled myself together. "Well, we can't have that, can we, Miss—?"

"Mrs., Doctor. Mrs. Hannah Browning. My husband thinks I might need glasses."

"We'll soon see about that. Sit here in the examination chair if you will."

She did as she was told, a meek little figure, except for that one outstanding feature. I adjusted my equipment.

"Tell me, Hannah—which seems clearer, A or B?"

"B."

I made another adjustment. "C or D?"

"They are really almost identical—but I guess C."

"B or C?"

"This is silly. I don't need glasses. I...I just came to make Bill happy. I think it's the stress. I've just had a baby, you see, and everything is at sixes and sevens."

I patted her shoulder reassuringly. "I'm inclined to agree with you, but I would like to run a few more tests. Let's go into the rear examination room." I gestured her before me, my heart pounding like a kettle drum in my chest.

She blindly obeyed—as I suspected she did all commands—and I surreptitiously turned the sign in the window from OPEN to CLOSED.

"These tests may take a while. Do you need to contact your husband and let him know you'll be late?"

"No, he's taken the baby to visit his parents. I don't expect them back before this evening."

"Perfect. I'd hate to rush the diagnosis."

"I'm all yours, Doctor."

25

The rear examination room was laid out for minor procedures like removing a splinter from an eye or dilation of the pupil. It would do nicely for my purposes.

"Lie down there on the chair and I will recline it for you. I'm just going to dim the lights so we can dilate your eyes—"

Hannah raised herself up on her elbows. "Is that really necessary, Doctor? Doesn't that take a while to dissipate? I did have other errands to do while Bill is out of the way."

"I assure you, my dear. It's perfectly normal and absolutely essential to my diagnosis." I kept my voice smooth and soothing with difficulty. The excitement was building in my chest.

I had everything planned out in my head. First, dilate the eyes—the huge pupils would enhance the remaining irises. Follow that up with the resin without removing the eyeballs from her head. It would be painful and maybe even fatal, but I had no intention of letting her walk out of here anyway. I would harvest the eyes and then drive her car to the airport as if she ran from her responsibilities. The body could be disposed of after dark with no one the wiser... All planned to the letter.

I turned back to the couch with the dilation solution in its syringe to find Hannah sitting up on the couch with a silenced pistol in her hand.

"I'm glad you flipped the sign to CLOSED, Doctor. Now there is no chance we'll be disturbed." She hopped down from the couch and gestured to it with the gun. "Take a seat."

"What the hell are you doing?"

She reached up and popped the brown contact out of her eye. "I knew the heterochromia would tempt you. I've done my homework, you see. Normally, I'd be fascinated by your hobby. But the boy in the ER? That was my baby brother. He caught an infection in the eye socket and died. You didn't need to harvest his eye. All the other doctors on duty thought it might be saved—but you were in charge, so you had the final say. I bet you have it displayed somewhere you can study it, don't you?

"I began looking into your history. Found out about your grandfather and how several families complained about the way their loved ones appeared after death. Discovered how animals near your boyhood home sometimes went missing, or turned up with an eye missing.

"I put it all together. And now I am here to put an end to it."

I stared, dumbfounded. I thought I had been so careful... "Hannah, listen—"

She pulled the trigger and there was an incredible pain in my left eye... just before the world went dark.

Watching

Justin Boote

Joe Brimsley walked into his bathroom, stripped naked and was about to step into the bathtub when he saw it. He recoiled in shock, slipped and banged his head hard against the sink as he fell. He rubbed his head and pushed himself back up again, looking for the thing in case it had escaped.

But it was still there, sitting in his bathtub as if defending its territory. The thing was hideous, a monstrosity that no God in his mind could surely have conceived while sober and rational. The multiple legs he could understand and reason with, even though the sight of the thing scurrying at breakneck speeds across his living room floor made his heart throb in horror and for gasps of terror to escape dry lips. That was just the shock of the sudden appearance—perfectly normal. But it was the other thing about it that he couldn't come to terms with. No matter how much he tried to rationalize, figure out a logical reason behind the anomaly, there never was one.

Its eyes.

Why the things had to have so many eyes was a terror that defied logic and belief. It must have come originally from some alien world, brought to Earth to cause equal amounts of disgust and despair because there was no way he could bring himself to admit that this was an invention of Mother Nature.

Its eight black orbs of insanity stared back at him, too. He knew this; the thing was watching him, studying him. Did it see eight different versions as though he was dissected for it to analyse separately before deciding its next move? He didn't know or care; all he cared about was that the thing was looking at him. Through him. Into him. He felt violated, as though his very soul was being inspected.

This, quite simply, could not be allowed.

Joe thought of flushing the thing down the drain but this wasn't a proven method—it could come back. It could come back and wait for him elsewhere. Under his pillow, perhaps or deep under the covers of his bed. He would climb into bed one night, feel something moving around in there and when he pulled back the blanket or lifted the pillow, there would be those grotesque, bulbous globes staring right back at him again.

Joe grabbed the nearest weapon he could find— a broom—and bludgeoned it to death. Then he flushed its remains.

***

The result of seeing a creature he hated so much brought with it the inevitable consequences. While he watched T.V. alone in his small apartment, things would magically appear and disappear out of the corner of his eye. Funny little itches and tickles on his body as he lay in bed caused him to scramble out in terror and lift all the blankets and sheets only to find crumbs. The next day, after killing the insect, he was again watching T.V., tired after a long day at the construction site. He was knocking back his fourth beer when movement to his left caught his eye. He turned quickly, already fearing the worst, and was shocked to see another spider sitting on the arm rest, facing him. His heart drummed against his chest, his lips peeled back, twisting into a grimace as instinct caused him to jolt and drop his beer bottle. He was sure he could see his reflection in those eight, black alien balls.

"You fucker!" He frantically looked around for something to obliterate it. He grabbed the beer bottle off the floor, not caring he was soaking himself from the remains, but before he could even raise the bottle above his head, the thing was gone.

"Oh no. Where the fuck did you go?"

There was nothing for it. He got up and lifted one end of the sofa, weapon in a white-knuckled hand, ready to launch it at the spider like a grenade, but it was gone. He dropped the sofa, pulled it out and searched along the back. Nothing. Impossible. There was no way the creature could have escaped so quickly despite having nearly as many legs as eyes. He knew there could be no peace at least for tonight; he would never be able to concentrate on the movie he was watching without seeing things again, feel those funny tickles on his bare legs.

He switched off the T.V. and went to bed.

His dreams were not comforting and peaceful.

When he awoke the next morning, he couldn't remember the exact details of his nightmare, only that he'd been sitting downstairs drinking a beer when something had tickled the back of his neck. When he rubbed it and looked at his hand he'd seen a spider sitting there. It was horrific because instead of having eight eyes in its furry head, it had a single, roving giant one instead. That blinked.

Joe didn't recall anything else but it must have been bad because a thin sheen of cold sweat was trickling into his eyes, making them sting. The blanket was hanging half off the bed so he had tossed and turned a lot and he was sure the wet stain on his underpants was not beer.

He took deep breaths, tried to focus on willing his heart to relax and rubbed a hand across his sweaty face. He looked up and stopped. His heart dropped a few inches again and began its manic thumping. He blinked and wiped his eyes hard, rubbing the sleep out of them. The lightbulb that he had never bothered to cover with a hade was not a light bulb any more. It was a huge, golden eyeball, complete with tiny red veins like bloodworms and a large red pupil like a perfectly formed drop of blood.

Joe whimpered.

He got up from bed and moved around the eye. It followed his gaze as if spinning on a dangling cable. Or maybe the cable was a long tendon; the eye belonging to some gargantuan creature up in the attic. Bile rose slowly from Joe's stomach from utter fright and shock. He thought briefly of touching it, but had the sudden certainty that if he

31

did, his finger would become glued to the gelatinous material of the object. He made a complete journey around the eyeball, followed at all times as it spun with him. He was still dreaming, of course—he had to be. This provided very little comfort.

And yet, at the same time, he knew this was really happening. He knew as surely as he knew that somehow this dangling eyeball was related to the spider he had massacred yesterday. He raised a trembling hand, tentatively poised to touch it regardless of whether his finger remained glued or not. They couldn't stand here all day looking at each other, but then he had a better idea. He grabbed a clothes hanger lying on his bedside table and turned around to poke it with that.

It was gone.

In its place was the grimy old light bulb.

Joe sat staring up at it, waiting to see if it changed back again, then finally looked down when his neck began aching.

"I imagined that. I was dreaming about that damn spider last night and of course I woke up with it still in my head. It's not a problem."

It finally stopped being a problem when he arrived at work and another gruelling ten-hour shift started.

After work, as usual, Joe figured several beers were called for. His best friend on the site, Carl, was already at the pub so he was alone. Tired, disorientated, he stepped into the road, leaping back when a horn boomed, almost scaring him to death. He saw a lorry's headlights: giant, blinking, golden eyeballs turning to face him as the lorry drove past.

Joe's jaw dropped. The memory of that morning rushed in with nightmarish qualities. telling himself it was a hallucination. He realised he was staring at other vehicles, scanning for more rogue eyeballs and praying he didn't see any.

Someone tapped him on the shoulder, making him jump.

"You okay, son?" asked an elderly gentleman.

"Huh?"

"I said, are you okay? You almost got run over there. You should be careful."

Joe stared into the man's rummy eyes, then backed away. There was something wrong with them. Something wrong with everyone looking his way. He felt some kind of freak. Joe ignored the old man and those glancing at him and ran to the pub.

He forced himself to calm down before going in. Maybe he was coming down with some kind of fever. He hadn't been feeling particularly well and had endured more headaches in the last few days than the previous three months. He took a deep breath, ran a hand through his hair on his head and walked in. A few beers would take care of everything - as always.

A few people looked at him as he headed towards the bar and, although triggering another squirming prickle of unease to crawl up his back, he ignored them. He saw Carl sitting at the bar.

"Hey, Carl, what's up?"

"I'm alright. Tired, but that's what the pub's for. What about you?"

"Yeah, getting too old for this shit. Bones feel like they're made of twigs." He took a long swig of his beer, then noticed a woman looking at him from the far end of the bar. On another occasion he might have taken it as a good thing—it had been too long since he'd replaced his ex—but she wasn't smiling. She was staring at him like the others outside when he nearly carked it..

"Are you listening?"

"Huh? What?"

"I said, you fancy a game of pool?"

Joe took another long swig, finishing his drink. He was about to order another when he saw the barman giving him the exact same glare. He turned around on his barstool. Everyone in the pub, some eight or nine people, kept throwing sly glances then looking away. Something was very wrong. He felt like someone who has some kind of ugly birthmark or big scar running across their face. Somehow he was attracting attention to himself and he didn't know why. More to the point, though, was that everyone looking at him was making him extremely nervous.

"Hey, Joe. The fuck's up? You ignoring me now or what?"

Joe turned and almost fell off his stool in fright.

Carl's eyes were the same colour and grim aspect as the light bulb in his bedroom, bloodshot to the point that no white was visible and the pupil was a dark crimson. A croaky whimpering sound came from Joe's throat as he stepped away. Everyone was against him, even his best friend. Conspiring against him. He was cursed. He had a tumour.

"The hell's wrong with you, Joe?"

"Don't come near me! You're part of it. You all are!"

Carl got off his stool. "I don't know what the fuck you're talkin' about, but I think you should see a—"

Joe pushed him hard and ran from the pub, aware that everyone was really staring at him—their eyes were burning holes in the back of his head.

"The fuck is wrong with me?" he asked again when he arrived home and dropped onto the sofa. The most likely suspect was a tumour or some such deadly illness, but the idea of going to the doctor filled him with just as much terror. Waiting around for results, considering the possibility that he might die. He was only twenty-three and while he might not have the most promising career and was often more lonely than not, that didn't mean he wanted to die. He had plans for the future, to finally overcome his natural reservations and shyness around women and get married one day. Visit some exotic country on holiday. Get a better paid job. He enjoyed playing around with computers and had ideas of running a web design company. If the doctor told him he had some great lump on his brain, he would have to come to terms with the fact that none of his plans were ever going to be fulfilled. Much better then to plead ignorance and pretend it wasn't there. But the more he thought about it, he was pretty confident a tumour had nothing to do with this.

It was something far more sinister and disturbing.

It had started after he killed the repulsive great spider in the bathtub. All those eyes. And now, lo and behold, he was seeing similar things everywhere he went. He almost chuckled at the thought and, if it wasn't for the gravity of the situation , he might have done, but was it possible for some sort of... curse to be put on him? Joe was superstitious, disbelieved the paranormal or anything remotely similar but something was happening here that required a broader imagination. If not, brain tumour or no, he thought he might go mad anyway.

If so, what was he going to do about it?

A search on Google offered very little, at least credible, on curses from animals, let alone insects, and he had to keep reminding himself why he was doing this. *Just how in hell was it possible for a stupid insect to put a curse on a human being?* It was ridiculous he told himself after an hour of browsing the Internet and reading the kind of stories that made him shake his head at such naïve, obviously coincidental occurrences.

So what that does that leave us with?

He thought of phoning his mother but she would insist he went to the doctor, too, and he really didn't want to do that, but the more he considered the alternatives, it became clear he didn't have too many alternatives. He threw down the phone in disgust and tried to concentrate on watching a movie instead. 'Pretend it isn't there and it'll go away on its own' was Joe's motto in life and that, he decided, would work here, too. Tomorrow was another day and the fever or whatever he had would be gone and things could go back to normal.

He smiled, settled back on the sofa to watch the movie, then happened to glance at the flowery wallpaper decorating the living room.

He recoiled and gasped in horror.

The flowers on the wallpaper were now blinking, golden, huge eyeballs, staring at him. The tiny red veins squirmed around the crimson pupils, blood seeping from the eyeballs as though the red veins really were worms scurrying down the wall. Hundreds of them looked back at him all around the room, a multitude of red pupils like laser-dots, roving left and right, up and down, as if inspecting their new home.

Joe jumped up off the sofa, spinning round and round, his terror increasing as the eyeballs followed his circling body. In his desperation, he tripped and fell over, landing very close to one of the walls. He turned around, eyeballs mere inches from his face, seeping blood. Tentatively, he reached out and touched one.

And screamed.

Instead of being a hard, solid wall, his finger started to sink into it, the texture and feel a gelatinous, soft membrane. Sobbing in despair and horror, Joe ran from the room and headed straight for the hospital.

Fortunately, the hospital was only twenty minutes away on foot. In near blind panic he ran all the way, screeching in terror as luminous, golden eyeballs followed his journey from those he bumped into, blood running in thin streams down their faces.

He burst into the hospital, almost barging an elderly lady out of the way.

"You gotta help me! The eyes. They're everywhere. I got a tumour and I'm gonna die. Help me quick, please!"

"Okay, okay, calm down," said the receptionist. "Let's start again. What seems to be the problem?"

"I keep seeing these huge, horrible eyes everywhere 'cause I got this tumour and everyone keeps starin' at me and I can't handle it. I don't wanna die, so you gotta get this tumour outta my head quick before I go mad or die."

***

"Mr. Brimsley. Joe? Hi, I'm a doctor. A specialist. The doctor who attended you has explained to me your… condition and what you believe is happening to you. I think I can help."

Joe looked nervously at the woman as she sat down. For now, her eyes were safe. Normal. He didn't know how long that might last but at the moment it was a good sign. He glanced outside her office, thin whimpers escaping dry lips as he saw all the other nurses and patients looking his way, their eyeballs huge and gleaming and red. All he could think about was how long he had left before the tumour in his head exploded like a water-melon.

"How long have I got, Doctor? To live? Be honest."

"Joe, listen. I'm the resident psychiatrist here. I've seen the results of the scans and you don't have a tumour. You're perfectly fit."

Joe stared at her, the words not quite sinking in. Maybe he'd misheard her or something, or this was some kind of sick joke. Anything was possible lately.

"Did you hear me, Joe? You have no tumour. You're not going to die. But I would like to talk to you about something else, though."

"I'm not going to die? You sure? You didn't get the results mixed up with someone else? I've seen it happen. It—"

"Joe, what triggered this... response to seeing eyeballs everywhere and reacting to how people stare at you?"

Shit. Now he really was going to sound mad if he told her about the spider, but...fuck it. He told her.

"I see. Would you say you are a very sociable person? Many friends?"

No, he wouldn't. He had never enjoyed being around large groups or crowds. They made him nervous, people staring at him all the time. Even at school he had dreaded having to stand up in front of class to recite passages or just simply talk. Joe liked to hide in the background.

He waited for her to start giggling or at the very least for a sly smile to cross her delicate features but she didn't. She stared at him for a while, took some notes, then looked back up.

"Joe, have you ever heard of scopophobia?"

"Nope."

"It's quite a rare disorder. A phobia that people suffer of being in crowds, of being stared at constantly. Usually it arises from childhood, being

39

constantly ridiculed in public and can manifest itself later after, say, suffering some kind of trauma or injury. You say you banged your head pretty hard after seeing the spider in your bathtub?"

"Yes," he said very slowly. What the hell was she talking about? A disorder? Phobia? Was he going to have to stay for an indefinite period in Northgate Hospital for the Mentally Impaired? Was he really a freak?

"It's nothing to worry about too much, Joe. With medication you can lead a perfectly normal life."

Yeah, right.

That night, he sat thinking about what the psychiatrist had said. He guessed she was right; he had always been a loner, resenting the idea of being thrust to the front of the crowd and his father had often belittled and insulted him when drunk. And it had to be better than dying from a tumour in his head.

Even though it bothered him to be labelled as a 'person with a disorder' it was far more comforting than be labelled as 'dead' in the next few weeks. He thought he could get used to the idea and if the medication worked, he could start doing something about his lonely, boring life.

Happy for the first time in days, Joe grabbed a beer from the fridge and was already contemplating how he might chat up the secretary at the building site once his meds kicked in. He stretched out on the sofa, absently watching some old action movie when movement to his right caught his eye.

Oh no. Oh no, please don't do this to me. I'm imagining it. This is not happening.

The spider, the huge, bloated creature that was the exact same size and species as the one he had mutilated, sat on the headrest of the sofa looking his way. Eight bulbous, grotesque orbs of black stared at him. Through him. He could see his reflection in those eyes and in those reflections he saw his own eyes, blood seeping from the corners with the crimson pupils glinting off the lightbulb above him, as they roved and bulged. When the spider took a step towards him, his reflection grew even larger until all he could see was his eyeballs, glistening in wet blood and about to explode.

Joe screamed. He quickly closed his mouth again when the spider had entered it and he felt the warm juices of its body running down his throat. The world went black as his eyes closed.

Don't Look

Dan Allen

"Let's go to Sicily," Meghan said. "We can visit your relatives and I know you'll love the food."

I'll tell you the truth about something. The food was fantastic. Some of the relatives I could do without. Especially the dead ones.

We took the ferry over from the Calabria region in the southern tip of Italy. On a big map, Sicily looks like it's a hundred miles away. But no. Bam, it's right there. Just a narrow strip of water and bingo. Hell, even a fat-ass like myself could swim it in an emergency. We landed in Messina. I remembered hearing the place mentioned in old war movies. You know, the ones with Nazis and stuff. My nonna was born and raised somewhere nearby, but I wasn't about to go stumbling around looking for ghosts. There were living relatives in Palermo, only a couple hundred kilometres away.

It was an interesting drive. You can enter a tunnel on flat ground and, three minutes later, you come out on a bridge a thousand feet high. Five minutes later, another tunnel and then another bridge. This time, two thousand feet in the air. I'm not exaggerating. Must've been over eighty bridges in total and twice as many tunnels. Halfway there, I got to thinking what an engineering marvel the whole thing was. Hell, back home, it woulda taken three hundred years to do this much roadwork. Meghan must've read my mind. She'd been sleeping with her head leaning against the door and snoring louder than the radio. Now, she clearly wanted to get my attention.

"Hey, Johnny."

"What?"

"Italians. They must be the greatest builders in the world, right?"

"Yeah, I guess."

"Then why haven't they built a bridge to Sicily?"

"I don't know. Jeezus, Meghan. Why you bustin' my chops?"

"Screw you, Johnny. It was just an observation." She put her feet up on the dash. There was a time when I thought that was sexy. Now it was annoying—stinky feet in my face.

"Down," I grumbled.

"You better slow down."

"What's that?" I played dumb.

"You're driving too fast. You're going to get a ticket."

Now I'm not sure if there was an actual speed limit on the A20 Autostrada or if one hundred and fifty km/h was just a suggestion. But either way, I hadn't seen any *Polizia* since we left the ferry and the few vehicles I saw usually passed in a blur. In Italy, nobody waits for you to get out of the way.

Finally we get to Palermo, see the relatives, eat the food, drink the wine. I've seen the Godfather twice. I knew what town I was in and, to be honest, I loved every minute of it. We wake up one morning and Meghan has this idea. She wants to see the catacombs. I wasn't overly keen about the whole thing. We'd spent over half of our vacation touring churches. I don't mean any disrespect. Italia has beautiful churches. You want to see beautiful churches? Go to Italy. The most magnificent in the world. I promise; you won't be disappointed. Anyway, Meghan was pushing and my Uncle Francesco whispered to me in Italian. Roughly translated, he told me to smile and nod. He said agreeing was easier than fighting. Wise man, my zio.

So, we go- crawling our way through the heaviest traffic on the planet to the far side of Palermo. Drivers ignore stop signs and a red light may mean slow down at best. Two lanes are quickly transformed into three and, when that's not enough, four. Pedestrians cross at will and risk their lives in a bizarre game of frogger. But the worst are the scooters zooming in and out between cars—dozens of them. No, make that hundreds. It is paralyzing to become concerned for their safety. Forget they are there and drive.

Catacombe dei Cappuccini. It wasn't what I expected. Sure, I'd seen catacombs before, but nothing like this. At the very worst, I imagined I might come face to face with an entire wall of stacked skulls, like in the tunnels under Paris, but this… Oh, my God, this was insanity. If it wasn't for the GPS, we might have never found the place and that would've been a blessing.

The entrance was a small door, barely visible from the street, marked with a hand-painted sign. In

Florence, the catacombs feature lavishly engraved marble slabs embedded into the most magnificent cathedrals' floors. But here, there wasn't a church to be seen. In hindsight, it made sense; there was nothing holy about this place.

At the edge of a small parking lot, a handful of tourists poked at the souvenirs, scarves and tee-shirts offered by a merchant. A canvas canopy protected him from the relentless sun, but it did little for the heat and the gipsy vendor earned his money. Beyond the door, an expressionless man sold tickets from a window beneath an arch and, to me, that seemed weird - paying to see the dead.

"How much?"

"Six Euros each," he replied in broken English. Perspiration dampened his balding head and gave his flesh a glossy shine. His expression changed and he looked like he had just tasted sour milk. I wasn't sure if it was the heat that annoyed him or if it was me.

I handed him a twenty.

"You have change," he said, more of a statement than a question and he waited while I fumbled through my pockets for a couple of coins. Satisfied, he handed me back a ten and a receipt. He reminded me of a restaurant mobster who once told me *I would eat whatever he was serving.*

A heavyset man, decked out in a bright red floral shirt, lime green short shorts and white flip-flops, brushed past me as if the train was full and about to leave the station. Being polite by nature, I was the one to apologize, but he ignored me and stuck his bulbous head in front of the glass.

45

"What is this place?"

"It's a retirement home. Whaddya think it is?"

The tourist shrugged.

"Six Euros," the ticket seller demanded.

I kept walking. Twenty feet further, a lady collected my ticket. Her job seemed unnecessary. Why couldn't the man in the booth just rip my ticket and send me on my way? I had little time to dwell on it. Stairs loomed ahead and Meghan was already on her way down. At the bottom of the first section of steps, the walls narrowed and the ceiling threatened to close in. My breathing increased in tempo and my heart raced to catch up. Of course, there were no windows and the lighting in the place was dim and flickered. Sometimes the lights would go out for a split second and I was seriously concerned they might stay off. Can you imagine, stuck in the dark with whatever was down there? I shoulda went back to the car right then, but no, that wouldn't have been cool. A big guy like me - you think I'm afraid of the dark?

Okay, no problem. But what about a cave-in? What if I'm trapped down there? Now, you gotta understand, I ain't no coward, but my worst fears were playing around in my head, messin' with my mind. I got a slight problem with something they call claustrophobia. Big word, I know. But it means I don't do well in small places.

I turned a corner and the next flight of stairs were much steeper and went down into the bowels of the earth. Right about then, I hesitated because there aren't any twinkle toes on my big feet. Hell, I have trouble walking a straight line even when I'm sober. I remember thinking if I missed a step or slipped a little... thumpity-thump, thump, bang, crash! I'd break my neck and be dead before I hit bottom. I spread my arms, pressed a palm against each wall and steadied myself as I tentatively took the first step. I didn't want to do it, you understand. I really needed to take a pass on this little adventure Meghan was already at the bottom. I couldn't look like no wussy in front of her.

So, like I said, I had no choice but to follow. I decided to sing a nursery rhyme to distract myself. Something about a spider and a waterspout: it probably wasn't the best choice, spiders and all, but at least it was a private moment and nobody heard me.

The stairwell emptied into a surprisingly massive room divided into a sporadic array of aisles. It was like being in a grocery store that sold dead guys. Hundreds of corpses were posed in a standing position and hung shoulder to shoulder along the walls, some two and three rows high. They still wore the remains of their burial clothes, dusty and moulded to their bodies. It was a gruesome sight, far more intense than any Hollywood special effects team could ever imagine. And trust me, I've seen some sick movies.

I was pretty blown away by all this, overwhelmed even. I walked down the closest aisle and kept my eyes straight ahead, so I didn't have to see any of these dead guys. They had them hanging like wallpaper. It was disrespectful. One face caught my attention, his eyes appeared to be looking right at me and I slowed down. I wasn't afraid; I just didn't want to rush into anything too creepy. Like a miniature mirage deep inside the eye socket, I saw the gloss of the man's pupil. Impossible, you say. I know it. I agree with you. So, I blinked and the pupil was gone, but the distinct shape of an eyeball remained. Okay, I'm not a stupid man. I know what a skull looks like. I should see large hollow orbital holes, but the tissue on this man's face had not fully decayed and rings of dried flesh clung round where his eyes should be. Skin continued halfway up the forehead and this friggin' guy, this corpse, he didn't look to be no four hundred years old. I remember thinking… those cobweb-like strands… are they the remains of his eyelids? I leaned closer, squinted and decided yes, they indeed were.

"Don't look at me, creeper," I muttered out loud and didn't even notice when the exact words repeated in my head.

Flesh covered the man's jawbone, dried out and all mummified-like and he had several remaining teeth- not all of them, but enough. Something sparkled. I took a closer look and smiled – a gold tooth! The Sicilian grave robbers missed one. It's hard to tell by the way I dress, but I know clothes and Mr Goldtooth here, he had some class and some moolah. His elaborate three-piece burial suit indicated wealth. Ash coloured and stained, I remember thinking that it may have been initially black and faded over the centuries, or it could have just as easily started white and turned grey with time. The jacket had nasty streaks from top to bottom and I wondered if his decaying flesh caused the stains or if they came from the ground where he

48

once rested. I didn't know then that none of these residents had received a proper burial and I assumed that some son of a bitch dug them up for display.

"My phone's dead. Let me see yours for a second."

Meghan's words startled me and I handed over my cell without thinking. Signs on every wall warned *No Cameras*. The flash went off and just before I blinked, I'm sure I saw fifty skeletal faces snap to look our way. Freaky, I know. And if I were certain, I would've left right there and then. But when you're in the middle of it, a little afraid, a little paranoid, you don't always trust your instincts.

"Jeezus, Meghan. We're not allowed to take pictures."

"Since when do you follow rules?" she sneered and handed me back my phone. "Besides, this guy is cute, with that one wonky eye. I bet he's not even real." She stretched her arm beyond the waist-high fencing and touched a sleeve. To my horror, his arm shifted a few inches from its posed position.

"Nice going, sweetheart. We'll probably get kicked out for that. I'm sure they have video surveillance everywhere."

"Oh, Johnny, you're such a bore." Meghan turned and wandered away, completely unfazed.

I hung back, still studying the details of this guy's clothing and trying to assess the century. A teardrop fell, presumably from the corpse, for there was no one else around and it landed by my foot. I know, right? I sucked in through my teeth and held my breath. Suddenly, I had an overwhelming urge to urinate. You know, take a leak. Once again, I studied the decayed flesh circling my deceased friend's eye socket and my rational mind determined that this was an impossible source for liquid. Hell, I wasn't crazy. Dead men don't cry. High above, I discovered condensation beading on the bottom of a pipe and I released the air held hostage in my lungs. I never did get to pee.

I watched Meghan turn a corner and disappear. I would've yelled for her to wait, but a dozen skull-like faces stared, daring me to make the first move. Don't let them know you're alone, I told myself. Don't let them see you're afraid. I kept talking, needing to coax myself through this crisis. If I wasn't careful, the dead would reanimate. I was sure of it. Like I said, paranoia will do this kind of shit to you. The room grew heavy, like an invisible weight pressing down on my shoulders. I felt profound hopelessness like there was nothing to look forward to. It's hard for me to compare that moment to anything else I've ever experienced, except maybe when I was a kid and my dog died. That was painful and I cried for a week. Anyway, I had to get out of there. I needed to find Meghan and leave this house of horrors. I specifically remember concentrating on moving one leg after another. Walk quickly, but don't make a scene.

"Look away," a man's voice said to my left. "Look away," another mumbled from my right, "Stop staring at me!" a woman's voice screeched, this time right up close and into my ear. More and more voices added to the chorus until hundreds were demanding the same. I covered my ears but still heard the echoes. With nothing to lose, I ran. I didn't care who saw me. The wife, other tourists, they would've run too. Trust me.

I found Meghan in the children's wing, staring at tiny bodies, some still in their coffins. A young boy, no more than six and still wearing his cap, hung on the wall beside a small girl, perhaps only half his age. She wore a dress, now filthy and rotted but once beautiful. All her front teeth were missing except for those long pointy ones, it gave her a horrifying smile. Anne Rice wrote something about vampire children. I believe she said it was forbidden to make one so young. Somebody didn't get the message. A chill swept over me. Now, I'm not poetic or anything like that. I experienced something icy, it woke me up and I felt ashamed. I realized I wasn't admiring a Halloween display. These were people. Even more disturbing, they were children.

How could they? I don't claim to be much of a church-going man. I'll take my mother to Mass now and then; unfortunately, I don't get much out of it. But this thing, displaying dead kids, it's an abomination. How could anyone possibly think God would be pleased? I swear, if someone had given me a flamethrower, I would've done the whole friggin' place.

I was getting worked up. There were strong emotions adrift and it was more than I could stand. I squeezed my wife's hand. "Do you want to leave?" I asked, hoping she would sense my distress and perhaps feel the same heaviness in the air.

51

"Not yet," she whispered. "I want to see the ladies wing, but you go ahead, chickenshit. I'll meet you at the car."

That reaffirmed my feelings regarding Meghan. She was a cold fish. Emotionally dead. I took a parting glance at the young vampire-like girl and the child appeared to turn her head ever so slightly, just enough to watch me leave. After everything I'd been through, it seemed normal.

I bypassed the remaining exhibits and reversed my steps towards the stairwell. There was a staleness I hadn't noticed before and my imagination worked up a list of all the diseases that may have killed these poor people. I pulled up my shirt and covered my nose as if that would save me from any airborne toxins. I refused to look when I passed the corpse with the functioning eyeball. But before I started up the stairs, I risked a glance back. The illusion, if that's what it was, remained intact. The appearance of an eye was undeniable, even to my once sceptical mind.

A wire snapped. Perhaps it was impeccable timing and maybe it was only coincidence that the wire in question was the exact one responsible for holding the well-dressed corpse upright, but I swear I saw the man stretch out his arms and lunge for me.

"Stop them," he said. "Stop them from looking."

It wasn't a whisper but more a shout, a demand. Sure, maybe I only heard it in my head, but I could smell his foul breath and taste the dust of decay. I panicked. I distinctly remember taking the Lord's name in vain, over and over again. I couldn't stand it anymore. The anxiety was too much and I ran up the stairs, carried by a mix of adrenaline and terror. I should've had a heart attack, that many stairs without a rest. Of course, I'm not in the best of shape either.

By the time I reached the top, breathing heavy and forcing one foot after the other, doubt was erasing fear. I've always had an active imagination and that, along with the claustrophobia... well, did I really see what I thought I saw? Maybe it was time to simmer down and have a glass of wine. A nice, chilled pinot grigio would do.

Outside, a young teenager sobbed and clung tightly to her mother. I understood the girl's grief and despair. This place was disgusting, built by men content to profit from the remains of the deceased. But their greed ultimately created something evil, something monstrous and like a sweating stick of dynamite, it was about to explode.

"Momma, it smiled at me," the teenager said.

"Baby, you know that's not possible. He's dead. Just a stack of bones." Tears glued clumps of hair against her daughter's cheek and the mother brushed them aside.

A rumble erupted and, at first, I thought people were arguing, but then the screams found their way up the stairwell. The tourist with the Hawaiian shirt burst out the door, holding his neck. Blood squirted between his fingers and rolled down his arm. Despite the remains of a sunburn, his face was white and he stumbled over his own feet and fell. One other person briefly made it out before something ungodly escaped. The ticket-collecting

53

lady slumped against the door frame and her hand touched the sidewalk before bony fingers dragged her back inside.

Screw this, I ran and imagined my moment on CNN, giving my first-hand account of how it all began. I planned to explain that the apocalypse wasn't caused by a passing comet or a germ-covered meteorite that just happened to land outside Jersey. Nor was it some flu virus or Asian pandemic. And it wasn't created by the government working on a vaccine or, lord help us, a new weapon. No, I would tell them, the zombie plague was all about revenge. I would preach about how we had mistreated the dead and how we had it coming. I would be in demand; appearance fees, book deals. I would get my fifteen minutes of fame, maybe more. Exhausted, I stopped running and wiped my forehead. I'm a fat guy. I needed a rest.

I'm sure the smile faded from my face when his ancient fingernails tore into my shoulder. I don't remember feeling his jaw break the flesh on my neck, but I did see a flash of gold and I knew it was him. Ironic, isn't it? I was planning on how I, too, could capitalize off the dead and bingo- I get my just deserts.

So, here I am, eating my way across Italy, one bite at a time. Not a bad gig, but the food is starting to taste all the same. The miserable ticket seller? Dead. Never saw him again. Meghan, my loving wife? She never got out either. I can only imagine what happened to her. Yikes!

Wonky crumbled to dust once he had his way with me. I found his suit right about where I landed

54

but no gold tooth. I can't explain that one. Maybe it was never there. I do still have his picture on my cell. Give me a shout and I'll let you see it. I'm not kidding.

Now I'm sure you want to know what happened to the Capuchin Catacombs. Well, some Sicilians know how to keep their mouths shut and cover up anything bad for business. God bless them. In just a matter of days, the place was cleaned and re-opened. Sure, it's missing a few regulars. Most notably old wonky eye, but there are eight thousand others to see. Look it up.

One last bit of advice. Despite how curious and eager you may be to see this dreadful place, don't go if you suffer from anxiety, panic attacks, post-traumatic stress disorder, paranoia, claustrophobia, depression, psychosis, schizophrenia, necrophobia, hell, any of the necros, especially necrophilia, nightmares, fear of paranormal activity, fear of the dark, fear of the dead, fear of the undead, fear of anything at all. Just don't go. The place is not a cemetery and it is far from peaceful. Nothing rests here and neither will you once you expose your fragile psyche to this evil madness.

Three Problems

Rickey Rivers Jr.

There's a small cabin in the forest. Inside the sound of clicking needles can be heard, a muscle memory rhythm. Aria is busy.

She is fond of the hobby, her new skill granted peace. It relaxed her, kept her sane, sane enough. The little home featured wooden floors that creaked, a ceiling that leaked and a fireplace, now cold, which could in fact warm the whole cabin. Indeed, a smaller word than quaint.

Books kept her company, but studying tired her and reading spells upon spells had gotten repetitive. She knew the value of the craft, but she valued peace much more. So it seemed almost to expect that the peace she enjoyed so much would soon be interrupted.

There was a knock on the front door. It didn't startle her. She had heard the would-be-delicate footsteps precede the knock. It was evident, the knocker meant to surprise. Regardless, she rose from her rocker and slipped one knitting needle into her brassiere, a trick she taught herself some time ago.

Aria went to the door and opened it and saw a sight she regretted. There he stood, as he had before, leaning, grinning; an unkempt mess of a man. His hair was ink-like, it covered his face and eyes, the red eyes; those damned red eyes. They

56

were hidden, yet they carried a presence. The past prodded and almost struck her in the side.

"Hey you," he said. There was smoke on his tongue. The smell of ash lingered. "It's been a while."

"It has," she said, as the smell caught her nose. "What happened to you?"

"Got caught with some dust, did some time. No biggie."

"Oh." It was all she could say. It made sense. What he said made sense.

"Aren't you gonna invite me in? I can't come in unless invited."

"You still abide by those customs?" She stepped aside, let him pass, bringing back old memories.

"Of coursc," hc said, "gotta havc standards."

Aria shut the door behind him. "Yet you walk in sunlight."

"That's for the skin, does a body well."

"Sure, for some."

"Yes," he said. "Some of us, my ancestors weren't so lucky, bad genes."

"Yeah, well, some things aren't bad, just different."

"You'd know about that." He pulled his hair away from his face and scanned the room with blood vision. His looked at the stack of books crawling up the walls. "Been reading?"

"Yes."

"Studying?"

"Yes."

He let the moment linger, cogs were moving within. "Witchcraft?"

"Once again, I say 'yes'."

"Unique! Who knew you had such hobbies?" Next he looked at the one knitting needle and the ball of fur next to it. "You knit too?"

"I knit too."

"Wow, you've changed, huh?"

She shrugged. Inside she tried to read his next move, an impossible thing.

"That's all good," he said. "I've changed too."

"Really?" she said. Why did she say that?

"Sure, been changing faces." He laughed his same laugh. The one she used to love.

"You clean?" she asked.

"Clean? Am I clean? Do I look it?"

She bit her lip, a foolish question.

He went on. "No, I get the urge every so often but I'm-oh, I-" He tilted his head and glared.

"What is it?"

"You've got a white streak in your hair."

She put a hand there. Age was a curse.

"It's like a blur of the moon at night. Time passes so quickly, doesn't it?" Every 'S' he spoke was like a snake's whisper.

She felt young again, dumb. He raised his hand to touch her. She took a step back. Another memory hit her like a slap in the face.

"Why are you here, Nathaniel?

He lifted his chin and inhaled. "That is quite the question. Maybe I wanted to catch up with an old friend."

"Well," she said, "we've caught up now. You can leave."

"So rude," he said, "so very rude." Nathaniel's gaze went from the cracks in her ceiling to the cracks in her face. Then the eyes were on her, those damned red eyes. Aria was frozen stiff. "I have a question. Do you have any dough, or even a few bucks?"

At that moment she felt outside herself. The eyes kept her in place, just like before. She saw herself standing in front of her own addiction, her affliction, Nathaniel, a drug of a man. She felt small in the now. If he wanted, he could do anything to her and no one would know. She was drowning, small in a sea of red. Her lungs were filling with salt, liquid salt. Blood was squeezing her eyes. A strangle pulled her further, further and further down. She couldn't see her cabin anymore. It was gone.

She told herself it wouldn't be like this, not anymore. Nathaniel was gone. He was supposed to be gone. She didn't need to be afraid, but she was. She was afraid he'd come back, afraid he'd ruin her life all over again. Why did she let him in? She'd been already weakened. What else was left?

Hope, she thought, hope *and witchcraft.*

A book within her mind revealed itself. It shone through the sea of blood. All at once the book opened and gave her the truth she needed: she was stronger than him.

Aria let out a scream. It was like catching fresh air for the first time in a long time. There was no fear in the scream, only hope, a small but powerful hope.

"No," she said. These words crept out, her lips moved in spite of her body.

Nathaniel took a step forward. "Only a few bucks, you know what I need."

"No," she said; the words of a ghost, swift, controlled.

"We used to get lifted together. Wasn't that fun? Don't you wanna do it again, just one more time?"

"No," she said again. This was her word. It felt lovely to say. She was smiling now, cackling.

"Come on, I know what you want. You know it too."

"Yeah, I'm off that stuff. I moved on. Unlike you, I grew up."

Nathaniel blinked, breaking the gaze. This gave her time, enough time to do what her mind had been screaming for her to do: she revealed the needle close to her heart.

He laughed. "Really now, you're gonna stab me?" Nathaniel stretched out his arms. A smirk crept across his face, a knowing smirk.

True enough she thought of stabbing, but knew better than to use physical force against him. Also true was the fact that the knitting needle had not been only a knitting needle.

"I'll give you another chance to leave, Nat, but if you don't, I'll have no choice."

"How much time has it been? You're really kicking me out? After all we've been through? Come on, put down that needle and join me for some dust. Trust me, you've love it."

She took a step back. "No."

Aria waved her wand and said the words fast, "into to the ground, mess of a man."

It was done as spoken. Nathaniel was laid flat, red eyes shining among flesh and organs. He lay still as vomit. The smell rose in the cabin. Chucks of him gathered into cracks of the floorboards.

Aria thought of less messy spells, could they have actually worked? The eyes came to mind next. She pondered a keepsake spell, much easier to deal with memories once the problems had been solved completely.

"Okay," she said, and readied her wand, "return you whole."

And the mess on the floor reanimated and returned itself whole again. Nathaniel stood once more, wide eyed and shaken. His face told a thousand year story.

"Orbs in skull," she said, "come hither."

And his eyes were plucked out, both falling into her waiting grasp. With another wand wave and a chant she returned him to the floor in a heap before he could even think to muster a scream. This time she liquefied him enough to fully seep between the floorboards.

"Wow," she exhaled. "That was pent up."

His ears overheard somewhere among the fleshy mess, floating below, not yet clogged by skin and fat.

Aria went down to her knees. The spells took their toll. She had never done four back to back before. Certainly not ones so powerful, they almost took her breath away, but she couldn't let him see that. Nathaniel couldn't know how stressful the

61

spells were. It would validate him, his scorn. She didn't want him to feel any higher than his current state.

For a while she remained on the floor gasping, one hand to her head. Then, after a while, she felt strong enough to rise again.

She had to clean the floor twice and air out the cabin for odors. After this she returned to her chair and knitting needles. Soon, the rhythm resumed. All had returned, even the stain beneath her. She kept the floating orbs in a nearby jar. She could do anything she wanted with them now. They had no power anymore.

At last she felt oneness. Never again would she allow the past to happen. She had blamed herself for far too long. Now there was pride, a worthwhile pride. She had overcome the pixie dust addiction. She had overcome Nathaniel, the addiction's introduction. And finally, those damned red eyes. None of them could harm her again. They were problems of the past. They were solved.

Seeing Is Believing, Isn't It?

Stuart Holland

They're watching you… they come out at night to check on us and they return to their hiding places before dawn. They crawl along the ground, climb walls and peer through windows on the lookout for their prey. Silently, stealthily, the red, bloodshot eyes pick their targets and apply the invisible markers of our destiny. Then, their mischief complete, they leave as silently as they came.

John Edwards was one of those targeted by the red eyes. He didn't realise it, of course, people rarely do, at least until it is too late. This particular night it was hot and humid and John left the bedroom window open his bedroom open. He fell into a disturbed sleep and never saw the eyes that climbed the wall to his bedroom. He was blissfully unaware of the red eyes that climbed through the open window and sprayed indelible drops of liquid on his forehead. Moments later the eyes were gone.

When John awoke in the morning he felt like he had the beginnings of a cold. The usual symptoms included a headache that seemed to get worse as he showered and shaved. Breakfast eaten, John made to leave for work. The painkillers (no brand adverts here) had failed to shift the feeling in his head. The front door closed behind him and the key was turned in the lock, though he was barely aware of his actions. It was purely his habits that were guiding him this morning. John took the half dozen paces to the sidewalk at the end of the front garden. He turned left as usual to walk to the bus stop and that was the moment when he finally realised something wasn't right. Suddenly he felt weak, his whole body collapsing under him. He was barely conscious when he sank to the ground, banging his head on the cold concrete. He tried futilely to sit up but John realised he couldn't see properly, nor could he move his arms which were like dead weights hanging to either side of his shoulders.

"Help!" He called out though no-one was near enough to hear his final, anguished cry.

And then he keeled over and collapsed in death. He never saw the eyes that were watching his final moments, peering out from the hedgerow across the road. Silently the eyes departed, knowing the next night they would select their next target.

The Watcher In The Well

Liam Spinage

For as long as I had been visiting my grandmother's rural retreat, there remained a singular object of fascination to me. It was an old stone well in the grounds at the rear of the property, overgrown with weeds. When I was younger, after scrabbling through the undergrowth to find it was the highlight of our summer visits. I would remain there all morning sometimes, my bare legs criss-crossed with tiny cuts from my adventures, much to the consternation of my doting mother who would undoubtedly sigh, shake her head and then apply just enough antiseptic to make me want to scream. I never did, though.

I had often imagined I could see eyes there in the depths, glistening beneath the waters, looking up through the lattice of the rusted iron grate which prevented me from clambering down the shaft. They terrified and fascinated in equal measure. I fashioned many stories to account for their presence. Mother seemed resigned to let these fantasies run their course.

They persevered, though, through angst-ridden adolescence. As an adult, I made tales of terror my stock in trade. The moderate fame granted me suited my quiet lifestyle well. Whilst I never 'made it big', they offered me a creative outlet after long days battling with support calls and the utter mundanity of office life. I was only really content when I closed my own eyes and saw those others staring back at me, unlidded and unblinking. Sometimes there was only a pair of them, staring at me over what I perceived to be a vast gulf of cold damp darkness. At other times, more would open to me. Tens, hundreds even. Watching. Waiting. Hungry.

I went back to that garden many times, not just to visit my grandmother. I even stayed there one summer when she was bedridden after a fall and I was nursing a bad break up and all the dramatic fallout that usually entails. Each time I went to the well and looked down, rapt in the unknowns of its depths. Always those eyes stared back at me, through me, beyond me. I even spoke to them on occasions, whispering lonely thoughts, dark secrets, hopes and dreams. I like to think that somehow they listened, that that's somehow how I got my first big break. A ridiculous notion, surely, but everything I am now I attribute to those slivers of light winking at me from the depths of the well, penetrating the cold iron lattice of the grate and up, up and away to the light of day and the tranquility of that overgrown garden.

Now, with the sad death of my beloved grandmother, the property was mine. I had been signing copies of my latest novel at a book fair when I heard. I had been so caught up in the fame of my new life that I didn't even know she had been struggling with cancer for two years. I tried not to let that detachment get to me, but I carried the guilt through the funeral in late autumn all the way through to signing the deeds in early spring the year after, right up to the moment I drove up to the house in the family Oldsmobile.

I was shocked at how much it had changed over the years. Perhaps my memory was playing tricks on me. I cast my mind back to the distant summer days of my youth, kicking my way fearlessly through the long grasses, turning over rocks to find new bugs to torment Mother with. The sun warmed my back as I watched my younger self on his bold adventure. Simpler, easier times, before the weight of the world and work took their toll.

Once I had taken inventory and had a list of everything I would need to purchase at the local store, I decided to set out on one further adventure of my own, to the furthest recess of the estate where the ancient, crumbling structure of the stone well resided. I had in mind to stare down the well once more, to gaze unafraid into the inky depths and find those eyes looking back at me once more.

Armed only with a rusty pair of secateurs, I cut a swathe through the thicket. It took me over two hours to make good my passage, by which time the sun was already dimming and the pale moon had risen to claim the heavens in its place. Finally I reached it, thirsty and exhausted. I leant on it momentarily to catch my breath and then peered over the edge as I had done in my youth.

Nothing gazed back. There were no eyes in the depths watching me. I made ready to return to the solitude of the house.

It was only later I realised two things which haunt me to this day. First, the grate which once covered the well was no longer there. Second, the grate was never there to prevent me from falling in. It was to prevent the watcher from climbing out.

The night I spent in that forsaken place was my first in many years. It would also be my last. It remains, boarded and bare, a legacy I am too afraid to claim for I had already gazed into that abyss and remain deathly afraid that one day it will find me and gaze back.

Professor Milverton Merely Observes

Jim Dyar

His name was Professor Clarence Milverton and to absolutely no one you are privileged to know about, he was The Eyes of the World. A man above all. A man of profound certitude. A man who rose promptly at 6 am with the absolute unbreakable knowledge that he had the world by the testicles.

By 6:05 am he had made his bed, aligning the sheets and coverlet with as close to perfection as the human eye could produce. By 6:15 he had showered, shaved, slapped his face exactly four times with aftershave and made his way downstairs where he ground his own coffee, boiled his own egg, made his own toast and spread it with a portion of the same brand of elderberry jelly that he had been buying since he was young and couldn't even imagine starting a day without it.

Professor Milverton had a certain amount of exactitude that ran through the fields hand and hand with his certitude.

"I can't stand another minute of him!"

"Can't you go to your parents' house, Clare?"

"No, the bastard would find me there."

By 6:45 Professor Milverton had finished his breakfast. By 6:50 he had cleared what he politely referred to as "his mess" all with the quiet air of a painted clockwork figure. By 7 am he had cleaned his teeth and selected yet another tweedy but dapper outfit from his closet. It was with an air of suppressed delight he began to adorn himself in what he considered simple but tasteful garments.

"I don't see how he's so bad."

"Of course, you don't, Mary Jane. He's Ugly! And not just facial ugly, but ugly all the down to his soul. I won't let him near the dog anymore. The poor thing has suffered enough."

By 7 am Milverton is going down the stairs and out his apartment building with a full Windsor tie. A newsstand on the way to the train station yields his morning glimpse of the world at large. He counts out the exact change with swift measured movements, ignoring the grumbling of other customers lined up behind him.

His slice of civilization purchased, he made his way to the train station, mustache quivering with the anticipation of the crisp folded newspaper. The next hour is spent perusing the articles and ads before arriving at Far Station, where he left through the gates heading for The Metroplex. It was a large building made of reflective glass managing to merely look imposing next to its more commercial brethren.

The lobby was largely empty apart from three security staff and a receptionist. He paused at the desk as they ran his I.D. The world was full of criminals and his staff didn't occupy more than one floor. Below and above his department were bankers and CEOs, speculators as well as other mercantile scum. A dozen businesses had their offices there, away from his precious systems and slightly worthy staff, of course. He'd never have agreed with this arrangement otherwise.

"Clare... what's wrong?"

"It's the dog. He killed the dog..."

Mary Jane gasped.

"I don't know what I'm going to do. He's in the den and the poor dog... He gutted her, Mary Jane. He took that poor animal and strung her up and..."

"You need to get out of there."

"I can't. Not yet. He's waiting for his dinner. If he doesn't get it, he'll come looking for me."

Professor Milverton had just stepped into the shiny chrome elevator when a voice barked for him to hold it.

Before he could turn around, a large sweaty man in a truly expensive suit hit the open button on the elevator door.

A break from his morning pattern simply wouldn't do. A crack in his facade had appeared. Displeasure was concealed by his quiet face and that simply wouldn't do. No one interrupted his schedule. He pushed the button for his floor as if the large burly man was more dangerous than a Bengal tiger.

"Well, good morning," the big guy chuckled. "Fancy meeting another human here before 10 am!"

Milverton smiled politely but said nothing as he meticulously moved his morning paper to his left arm almost as if it would somehow become a barrier to human interaction.

He was aware of the big man as well as his reputation, not that he had ever met him or ever seen him before in the building. Across the big screen of his mind's eye, the professor saw a series of ledger notes. Money moving between banks, a two-hundred-foot yacht, blue smoke and mirrors to his clients and the small and untimely death of a fifteen-year-old girl that had never been solved.

If Milverton was the sort of man who had the imagination or the compassion to do the right thing, the large sweaty brute would be a pretty red stain floating in the shark-infested froth just off the side of a burning lifeboat but Professor Milverton had been hired for his clockwork lifestyle, his devotion to computer code and his singular lack of imagination. He was a legend among the NSA elites and he had never strayed.

Well. Maybe once. But love makes people crazy sometimes.

The officer studied the phone carefully.

"You said you received this text from a divorce lawyer that just happened to want to help you out?"

Clare nodded, staring at the cooling pool of blood her late husband was leaking into the living room carpet. Earl had put up a struggle but had clearly not been ready for the savage stabbing that he had taken. It looked like every knife in the entire kitchen had been used at one point or another. She could only imagine the flight of terror he had made trying to escape.

The officers were imagining it too.

"Did you notice, ma'am, that this text is from your own phone?"

Clare stared at the officer, dumbfounded, as he showed her the phone. A clink behind her alerted

72

her that the other officer in the room had grabbed his cuffs.

"What are you doing?"

"It's just for your safety, ma'am. Please don't make more of it than it is. We just need you to come with us and regulations say we can't have anyone in the back of the car without cuffs."

Clare stared at them in horror. The first officer gave her a warm smile as things slid well out of control.

"Do you have anyone who can collaborate your story?" the second officer asked earnestly and listened politely right up until the cuffs were on her.

Professor Milverton settled at his desk with a slight smile. He had a stack of reports in the in tray, meetings to attend, A.I.'s to train, requests to file, priorities to attain and a global network of cameras to scour for traces of terrorist activities, but he always started and ended his day peering at Clare's cell. Watching her eat, watching her sleep.

Keeping her safe.

Professor Clarence Milverton would never dream of meeting the love of his life, for like the machines he monitored and the network he controlled, he too was a thing best obscured by shadows.

How to Read a Woman

SJ Townend

Freckles: dot-to-dot maps which contained the secrets of the future. Each woman was an unread book. The patterns on a lady's skin would unearth a story. This was his form of astrology. He'd taught himself to read in this way and it is what he believed and knew to be true. Only by connecting the beauty spots and pockmarks on a woman's skin with lines, with the rich red stretches a blade would proffer, could he see the prescient constellations dictating his own future clearly.

In his bag he carried a variety of tools to help him bisect his next piece: a razorblade, a scalpel, a steak knife, a hacksaw, an axe.

Cheek by limestone jowl, he sat amongst the darkness, between the pressing faces of the towering walls of the empty university buildings. He waited under the watchfulness of a strong moon. He was sure he would find someone suitable— young, marked—and her skin would give him what he needed. No idea yet who she would be, he knew the darkness of the night would deliver. He sat tight. With only the deserted cityscape, his rucksack of bundled blades and the ceiling of yellow light pollution for company, he waited—hidden—near the night club. It would open soon.

Cars started to pass rarely and then frequently. The little hand on his watch crept closer to eleven.

Taxis spilt groups of Friday night revellers, loosely drunk and high on their own youth and everything else the city had to offer. The night smelt for them of pheromones and hope. For him, soon, he hoped, it'd smell of coppery vermillion; nothing was quite as fragrant as the pages of a freshly-skinned book.

He watched from his crevice for the right one. This dive of a student club was a gamble, but he had no better place else to be. A people-carrier pulled up into the taxi rank a few feet from the entrance, a stone's throw from his watchful glare and, solo, out she stepped.

His green eyes sparkled with the light of Lucifer at the sight of her. This would be his takings, for sure. He could not wait to cut and slice from her the narrative of her very spirit. What stories would the map of her skin markings reveal?

She was wearing a black dress with a zipper running down from neckline to hemline. Auburn curls tumbled from her high ponytail, the skin on her exposed arms and legs as translucent as rice paper, as thin and as marked as pages from an old bible. He stretched his neck to watch her strut into the club, ever careful not to reveal himself too soon—he needed her drunk first, intoxicated, so he could have his wicked way. His heart revved and pumped fast blood laced with expectation to his keen fingers and toes. Her skin was laced with prophecy. She'd keep him busy. What a read this one would be.

***

Three hours passed. She stumbled out through the safety net of bouncers and then alone, into the mouth of the night. Would she call and wait for a taxi? Would she walk the half mile to the kebab shop, the only remaining source of food in the city at this ungodly hour? He watched with bated breath.

With his bag swung over his shoulder, he scuttled between the shadows behind her. She walked past the empty taxi rank and, staccato-heeled, tip-tapped around the corner. This was his chance to approach, not a soul other than the pair of them present.

"Excuse me, madam." The slip of a girl, early twenties, skin of treasure, turned around to face him.

"Hello."

"Saw you in the club. Was going to buy you a drink, but you left before I'd the chance," he lied. He'd never set foot inside of that boom-box building of noise and promiscuity. He was not the partying type, more the studious type, always reading. He preferred to while away his daylight hours alone, at home, amongst his library of hung-flesh fiction. "Hope you don't mind me approaching you like this—"

"No. Not at all," she interrupted. This took him aback. He could not smell fear permeating from this one's beautiful skin. He enjoyed a challenge. He would make her feel fear. He would enjoy watching the colour drop from this one's cheeks. "I'm Lamia. And you are...?" She moved closer. He clutched his bag. Even in the moonlight he could see threads of purple veins running under her skin. He could trace

76

the ribbons of blood vessels snaking around underneath crops of freckles.

"I'm...." She did not need to know his name. He changed the subject. "Would you like me to escort you home?"

"How very gentlemanly—that would be divine."

She pushed her thin arm through the loop of his. A stream of pleasure shot through his very core. His eyes darted around the translucent, bespeckled skin of her arm wrapped in his as she recounted the non-events of her evening. He didn't hear a word she said. In his mind, he was already slicing through her cold body, connecting the largest, protruding moles he might find first with his fingertips, like Braille, with a simple razor blade to provide a sketch of his future, an outline. Then he would hack through this framework with his axe to split the parts of the story her body would reveal. Once separated into chapters, he would wipe away her red ink and join the smaller brown and orange marks which decorated every visible part of her skin with the steak knife or scalpel. This would reveal the beauty in the sentences of each page of her flesh.

"So this is me." She delved into her purse for her key. "It's been lovely chatting. Divine. Would you care to come in for a..." Her eyes mocked coyness. She bit her lip playfully.

His eyes flitted left and right and behind to check they were alone on the steps of her apartment. This was all too easy. Adrenaline flushed his cells at the thought of the joys that were to come, the pages he would turn.

"Yes. Yes I would. That'd be... divine," he said, too distracted to select new words of his own.

He followed her up the steps. He traced the star-charts of the heavens that scattered in freckle-form over the backs of her legs.

***

"Tea or wine?" she called from the kitchen. He sat perched on the edge of the sofa. Where would he place the pages of derma once he'd ripped apart the story of this redhead?

She came back in with an opened bottle of Malbec and two glasses.

This one would whiten with fear, he thought. All colour from her flesh would vanish. Her face, round like the moon, would pallor. The dusting of freckles on her cheeks would pop against the ashen canvas. He felt himself harden with excitement as he took the glass from her.

Whilst she'd been out in the kitchen, he'd sequestered his tools: the axe lay hidden beneath the sofa cushion, the steak knife was tucked in the cuff of his boot.

"You've beautiful eyes," she said and perched next to him. Her bare leg skin brushed against his knee. Ecstasy, he felt.

"Thank you," he replied. "And you have beautiful skin."

"You've seen nothing yet." Her fingertips took the zip which lay above her delicate décolletage. "Would you like to see more?"

"Very much so." His night was about to peak, his future about to be revealed, He felt for the weapon between the cushions. His other hand was placed on her knee and traced upon it a small crucifix patterning of freckles. Further up her leg, his index finger slid over a stretch of pigmentation, age spots, which curved round like a scythe. Old Father Time. He pressed on the curve of her hip. The girl was an hourglass. He couldn't wait to carve and connect the grains of sand which lay speckled on her skin.

She drew down her zipper. He drew up his weapon.

She peeled open her skin tight dress. A scream ripped from his throat. His face, stamped with the mark of terror, could not believe what she had revealed. Before his own eyes were tens, a hundred more eyes. Blues, greens, browns and all shades of hell in between.

From breast to pelvis, myriad eyes burst out from her skin; clusters and patches of eyeballs, small and large, lashed and not. Some ogled side-by-side a matching partner, some bulged alone, others blinked centrepiece, encircled by more. Where her nipples should've been were irises of red, pupils like black holes. The eyes blinked and twitched like faulty Christmas tree lights. Pupils dilated and flitted around the room before all settling forwards on him.

"Your eyes," she said. She draped her slim arms around his thick neck and pulled her face closer to his. Her crimson lips spoke two inches from his face. "I need your eyes." She pressed her lips against his and stared directly at him with the eyes on her face. She gripped and forced open his eyelids so he could not close away from the terror of her. Her eyes held the suction power of an oceanic drain hole. They yanked out from his sockets the lashes and the lenses first and then the white scerla split apart like an egg cracked. Her full lips slurped the eye juice and it trickled down inside her. The fluids within his orbital sockets sprayed out onto her face, each drop was absorbed through her translucent skin. Like water down the plug hole, his face and body became sucked up and through her infinite pupils, portals to the underworld, doors to the outskirts of the universe.

In the blink of an eye, he was gone. She sat alone on her sofa.

The girl felt the familiar tickle, this time on her inner thigh. Two dark moles of the warty variety had been there before; now two new green eyes were rolling through. The visionary opals throbbed and blinked against the top sheet of her paper thin skin until, like miniature volcanoes they erupted up and through and out from her flesh. The surface of the skin on the thigh crowned his green eyes opening, full of emerald lava and fear.

She zipped her dress back up and rubbed each of her sore eyes through the fabric, they had seen enough for now. Satisfied with all her accomplishments of the night, she finished off her wine.

The Chill of Her Disdain

Dona Fox

Another belly lurching jolt buckled my knees and tossed me onto the beach; my helpless body reminded me of the games I played with my mommet of Mama.

I dug burnt fingers into the black sand and pools of water filled the holes.

Intended to be our salvation, the island was sinking.

Squashed bug-flat to the shingle, I crawled to the frothing water line and sorted through the charred debris of our private jet as salty water filled my mouth with guilty tears.

My fault. I wanted to tease Mama, share a joke between us, make her smile with me. It was my birthday. I hadn't thought she'd go mad and bring the whole plane down. I tried to stop her, to tell her, but oh, her eyes–that look.

I fell soft on the beach; the rest of them fell hard, spiraling down like candles as I, wishless, watched their bodies lodging deep into my sandy cake–the island–my only birthday cake.

The plane followed a wonder of fireworks and light fiery dragons danced for me and burnt my lashes–like the best birthday ever–not. My every party dress ruined now.

Perhaps the weight of the airplane set it off. The island jolted like the elevator had last week.

The big red button—emergency stop. Hilarious until she slapped me. She liked her parenting quick and hard. I should have known she'd freak about the plane.

I stick bits of debris into the sand at the high tide line then I crawled away to find Mama's body. I would tell her I hadn't meant for it to go this far. I'd say I'm sorry for stopping the elevator, for making [and using] the little mommet of her, for causing her to crash the plane and for all my other faults, all the horrible things that are so wrong with me.

The setting sun revealed dozens of lumps beneath the sand.

I'm sure it's the others in their shallow graves, just beneath the grains.

They are moving!

Perhaps I'll have company before the night hunkers down.

I'm so afraid of the dark. The darkness sets me off, you see. Creatures are hiding in the swirling grains of night. When I'm alone, that's when they peel back my hair and lick the hollows of my ears.

I won't be alone when the ocean sweeps us off the land.

Mama used water as a punishment.

I don't like being under water. The water is alive, you know. We came from water, not from dust. There are hands in the water, mean hands.

Quick, I scrabble as the ground trembles and another jolt holds me flat again.

I pause.

What if I dig to save another and the hole fills with water, as does every impression my fingers make into the sand? I picture the ocean under this thin film of black grains, watching for its chance, reaching, holding the island in its briny fingers, squeezing it slowly like a sponge.

What if I dig down and tickle that watery palm? What if the sea gushes through? Will the island sink faster?

How horrible of me to think such a thing—weighing the rescue of another against my fear of water.

Filthy arms of foam reach from the waves that sneak onto the beach, then frothy legs stretch like ballerinas, readying to dance on tiptoes across the sand. The water dancers are spinning toward me.

I hurry to the closest mound and dig until, strangely, my hands find the space is filled with nothing but the swirling sea. I pull away from the watery hole I've dug and plant my toes into drier sand.

The sun has set and all is darkness on this sinking land—and, as the shadows begin to swirl into bizarre shapes, a slimy force captures me and draws me to itself and the void sucks me down.

The sides of the hollow are very close. Steaming bubbles shoot past me; as I fall, the water in the tube grows warmer. This beast of an island is swallowing me. I cannot move, for panic has frozen my muscles and my heart beats in my temples.

A rising body jostles me.

Mama's come to save me.

I grab hold of the soft flesh. Soon we break the surface through the opening I made. I push it out then use the body's weight to pull myself to freedom.

I lay on the sand taking vast gulps of sea air, then I begin gasping, gagging, coughing and my throat burns hotter than my eyes.

It's dark now, but the stars are brighter than any stars I've ever known.

Then I examine the body; her wet clothes are black, burnt, and shapeless. I push back her hair, touch her skin and peer into her swollen eyes.

The body moves.

Steaming water pours from the corpse's mouth.

This is not my mother.

I look across the sand. There are other lumps; some are belching open. I will spend the rest of my life searching for Mama's body. I will devise a penance acceptable to her. I will consume her raw to give her life again, my life. She will live through me if that is what she wants if that is what it takes to please her.

I scream at the sky, at the ocean, "Mama!" and my need tears the lining of my throat.

I turn to look back at the waves, but that's not necessary; the water dancers are writhing at my feet. They have come well past the high tide mark; proof the land is going down.

The island quakes. I fall to my knees. The dancers stream across the sand in rivers, jump over my head in waves of cold fury, yet as they withdraw, they scald me with their boiling feet.

I rise in pain to see a fiery mountain bursting up from the sand and tides of brilliant orange lava creatures streaking toward me, mimicking rivers of orange fire. There is no escape; millions of them race across the sand to the ocean.

As the lava comes to entomb me, the rest of my life appears to be foreshortened; if I had found Mama, there was much I wanted to whisper in her dead ear that I had not been free to say to her indifferent one.

It was not so much blatant censorship as simply the fact that, over time, the chill of her disdain froze all voices but her own.

She never knew me.

She might have loved me.

I sing my tale into a sea shell, a wisp of memory you imagine when you hold it to your ear, mistaking my song for the ocean's roar; feverishly, I carve my story into the dampened sand to be found beside my bones, beneath the hardened lava.

Look At Me

Olivia Arieti

The eyes first met while swinging up and down in the school's courtyard; the glance was quick, childish but memorable. They had fallen in love; theirs was puppy love actually, a cute prelude to what was to come. No time to talk, a wink the only goodbye, then back to one's own classroom... Years passed, mates changed, but the pupils remembered and when in the hustle and bustle of the high street they met again, immediate was the joy; the mouth smiled and they twinkled with that special light that belongs to lovers only. The vision was instant though; the bodies were pushed away and once again the eyes lost themselves and darkened for the colour of nostalgia had entered the irises. The only comfort had been supplied by recognition, their ability to discern among hundreds the ones that had first impressed them; since then, it became the strength that made them carry on till the next encounter.

It took place on a bright spring day when the tender rays had been captured by the lens tired of the sullen wintry greyness. Rebirth and reawakening filled the air and the eyes were relishing the miracles of the season's pastels. The mouth smiled again, the faces moved close and the lips kissed; the image was jealously treasured, forever a precious reliquary.

They never tired of gazing at one another, as though the sight might vanish. Love irradiated the irises with the shades of passion and desire and the eyes gleamed endlessly night and day, animated by enduring romance. No touch could have been as burning as their gaze.

They talked about the present and glowed feverishly when wondering about the future, constellated with dreams and mirages. Foreseeing ranked among their most pleasant pastime and the anticipations were more than enchanting.

It was then that something went wrong and the fire that had brightened them like the highest flames of the hearth, suddenly went out. They turned dim, all visions blurred and, unable to talk any longer and bear the blameful and condemnatory looks, hid under the eyelids.

By now they eluded each other; the glance became challenging, almost frightening. Sneers, mocks, insults flashed across them and fearful that their sights, perhaps too sinful or daring or squalid might be spotted, they lowered or turned away unwilling to disclose the most intimate layers of the soul. The dread made them wild and intermittent flashes of madness were visible. Horror, too, had entered the pupils' holes with the blackness of evil.

Tenderness and warmth had totally dissolved and a gelid glare replaced the caring gaze. Departure was better; sunglasses helped. No tears were shed; all images whether reveries or mirages, had lost their poetry, love had deteriorated and dullness made all colours gloomy; no more suggestive sunsets, blossoming dawns or blue horizons, no more excitement or resplendence. Dark, ominous semblances that impeded to rest even when they were closed, intruded on their privacy. Strained and sore, they had to look elsewhere.

They embraced other spaces, fixed on other eyes, young and old, desperate and happy, sly and loyal, yet it wasn't easy... Focusing on the unknown wasn't as fulfilling as expected and something was always missing. A horrible mistake had been made.

The glance became wistful, even sad, it started wandering up and down, side to side, looking back but the path was deserted except for the eerie shadows of what had been missed like the void of the dead, shapeless and colourless, but infinitely painful.

Quite often, the eyes reddened and swelled as if punctured by needles, the pointed shards of the fractured images longing to be recomposed; otherwise they were overwhelmed by regrets that, too heartrending to keep inside, took the shape of tears and inundated the cheeks.

"Where are you? Look at me..." they cried, implored, but wherever they turned there was no trace of the beloved ones.

Blankness had become a ghastly perception carved in infinity, an extension of time too long for them.

***

Other seasons passed before the final reunion, so amazingly overcoming that the eyes nearly popped out of the heads. Too bad one was dead. A lethal accident out of despair. Now a vitreous little ball filled the bony cavity, like a marble, rigid and fierce in its immobility. It didn't matter, though, for the surviving one had gathered all its previous partner's intensity, light and perceptions.

The eyes promised never to depart; a silent indissoluble tie had been impressed in the pupils.

Tears were spilt, the single eye crying for two. They would never lose themselves again, always together... till death. The awareness made them shine with a celestial luminescence as though already in heaven, a gentle soothing glimmer that reflected on the whole face.

Aging and the decreasing sight were no impediment for now they could see beyond, all three of them. Secrets had been revealed, offences deleted and nothing left to conceal... True, there was less excitement, but far more peace necessary for the last wait.

Most of the time semi closed or entirely shut, they went through their most glorious images; when they reopened, the loving glance would rest on the one before them and they would twinkle feebly but happily.

The single eye survived the others that closed softly before springing wide open. It cried a whole night and day; the marble-like one, of course, remained impassive, but the violence of the sobs made it shake in its socket.

The tears had been so abundant that they caused a severe problem and the only existing eye turned red, then dark and finally lost all light.

It remained alive for long, even if blind like the vitreous companion, but it didn't care for there was nothing more to see.

Those Eyes Are Mine

Justin Boote

Henry Robertson rubbed his eyes again to clear the blurriness from them, knowing no matter how much he rubbed, it wouldn't make much difference. And he really needed it to. The man he was stalking was going to get away if he couldn't see properly and, more importantly, ensure no one saw it happen. He wanted to get a clearer image of his face, specifically the eyes; this would determine whether he was wasting his time or not, but now, the way things were, Henry could hardly do that.

He watched as the hazy figure walked down a dark alleyway and followed quickly behind him. When he was as sure as possible no one else was in the vicinity, he pulled the heavy hammer from his coat and smashed the man over the back of his head. He crumpled to the floor without so much as a groan. Henry dragged him behind a large set of rubbish bins and got to work. He turned him over and raised his eyelids. It was hard to see in the dark but the man had blue eyes, just like his. Perfect.

Henry removed his large knife and deftly and carefully set about cutting out the man's eyeballs. It was a highly delicate operation but he'd had enough practice now to almost consider himself an expert. But then, just as he was about to start, giggling voices came from further down the alley. Horny kids, no doubt. He cursed and was forced to work fast which would almost surely guarantee a failure or mistake. He waited with bated breath to see if the couple came closer and was relieved to see them at the far end, caressing and kissing against the wall. There was absolutely no way he would allow himself to be caught doing this; he'd kill himself rather than go to prison.

He finished the job rapidly, then once they were removed, he wrapped them in soft tissue and placed them in a small ice box he carried with him for the job.

Now he was looking at the unconscious man lying on the ground, a sense of pity overcame him. It had never happened before; he considered his needs far more important than those of others, but it occurred to him for some reason that this man might have a wife. Kids. Was he really going to let him wake up, find out he was blind and leave him to continue the rest of his miserable existence in this state? Henry knew all about miserable existences; he'd been living his own for the last six months.

Normally he didn't care but perhaps the urgency of his own existence—and maintenance of—was finally getting to him. The desperation.

Henry squatted beside the man and, checking once again to make sure the couple were occupied, he eased the knife deep into the victim's heart. A weak groan blew from the man's lips and he was dead. Henry left as quickly as possible and headed towards the surgeon's home.

***

Henry threw his empty beer bottle across the living room. Another complete failure. Tom, his surgeon friend, had given him some complicated technical speech again about optical nerves, retinas and muscle tissue which he didn't understand. All he had understood, for the umpteenth time, was it wasn't going to work.

It had to work.

His life depended upon it.

"Why the hell does it have to be so difficult?" he yelled at the empty house. "All I want is to be normal. Is that so much to ask?"

When he had first visited the doctor and told him his problem, he had been referred to a specialist who had said it was virtually impossible to cure. Science just wasn't advanced enough.

"How much?" he had asked.

"How much for what?"

"I'll pay. Money solves everything so tell me what it will cost. I have the money."

"It doesn't work like that. You can't fix things when you don't have the tools to do so. We can try an operation on the retinas to slow down the process, but for now, that's it. No amount of money will cure you, Henry. I'm sorry."

But Henry had insisted, said they had to try. He would kill himself first, rather than suffer this way. He also hinted he would kill Tom, his surgeon friend, who he visited next, too, if he didn't at least give it a go. That helped.

He meant it. When he had started suffering longer and longer bouts of blurry vision, he knew something bad was happening. Then the headaches started. Up to six months ago he not suffered migraines; now they were every other day. When he found the courage to go to the doctor, his fears were verified; he was going blind. In less than a year the world would turn black for him and there was no chance of a recovery.

"I am not going to go blind," he told himself yet again. It had become his mantra. There had to be a way. Every time he took a set of eyeballs to Tom, he was told the same thing; refusing to even try and operate on him.

He fetched another beer from the fridge, having to hold it up close to his face to make sure it wasn't something different. His eyesight was fading rapidly, something needed doing. But even as he contemplated the situation, the solution occurred to him. And really, it was so easy; he wondered why he hadn't thought of it before. Tomorrow night would be the last. Whether Tom liked it or not, he was going to do it. He would be able to see for himself Tom's operating skills.

***

To pay for the eventual operation, Henry had sold his house and moved into a cheap apartment, barely furnished. If it didn't work, he had every intention of ending his life anyway so right now material belongings were irrelevant. The police were looking for the murderer of four people, all with their eyeballs cut out and sooner or later they would catch up with him. If the transplant worked, he had enough money to get out of the country and start elsewhere. He woke up on the sofa that doubled as a bed, made himself a coffee and prepared to leave under the cover of darkness. This time he would have to take his car which was dangerous, considering he could hardly see, but there was nothing else for it—the risks would have to be taken.

When his clock chimed twelve p.m. he left the apartment and made his way to his car. He fumbled with the lock, finally opened the door and climbed in. The police may be looking for a vicious, cruel murderer but they didn't seem to be looking that hard for him. He drove to the same area as always, slower than usual, over near an industrial site with very few people about but where the local prostitutes made their income. There was always someone hanging about the place alone, perhaps building up the courage to hire one of their services.

A police car drove slowly around the warehouses, flashlight beam emanating from the passenger side, then drove off. Nervous yet excited at the same time that it might finally be the last excursion, he waited until he was sure the car wouldn't return then drove closer to the prostitutes. There, over by a street corner, was a guy by himself, leaning against a wall, looking highly suspicious. Not wanting to appear as a plain-clothes officer and scare him off, he drove around the site until he came up to the man from behind and parked by the corner.

Henry grabbed his hammer and stepped out the car. His heart was thudding madly in his chest. He couldn't quite tell in the dark from once more blurry vision but the guy seemed pretty big—his shadow stretched over the street, long and wide like some gargantuan creature. Henry raised his hammer, got as close as he possibly could when the man turned around. He never even attempted to run.

Henry brought the hammer down hard on his skull.

Sure he was on the verge of a heart attack, panic soaring up his body, he dragged the man over to his car and dropped him to the ground.

"Come on, come on. Where the fuck are they?" He couldn't find his keys. He rummaged through his pockets, then a second time. He'd dropped them, must have done while creeping up on his victim. He was about to rush back to where he'd hit him when he remembered the keys were still in the car, the doors open. He cursed under his breath, then opened the back door and somehow managed to push the huge guy in.

"Thank God for that," he muttered, checking to make sure no one had seen him or was watching. "Right then, Tom, time to get to work." He drove straight to Tom's house, smiling knowing that this time, nothing could go wrong. By tomorrow he would have the best eyesight imaginable.

"What the hell are you doing?" cried Tom in his pyjamas, half-asleep when he opened the front door.

"This time, Tom. And there's no backing out of it. We do the operation now or I swear to God you won't live to see another day." Henry pulled out his trusty knife to prove his threat.

"But it can't happen, I told you. The optic nerve. Muscle tissue. Once severed, it's useless."

This was bullshit. If they could do heart transplants they could do eye transplants, too. Tom was just too much of a coward to want to do it.

"That's why this time you're going to do all the hard work. You can cut the nerves or whatever yourself. The guy's in the back of my car. Let's go."

Tom stared at Henry wide-eyed, bottom jaw bobbling up and down as he tried to speak. Henry didn't care. He knew about Tom's addictions and had proof if necessary. If Tom failed to comply, a quick phone call to the police and Tom would lose not only his license but his freedom for a few years. Tom had been made perfectly aware of the fact.

They drove in silence to Tom's private makeshift surgery, apart from the guy in the back starting to moan and groan. Henry drove faster. Once there, they both dragged the man quickly into the surgery and strapped him to the operating table.

"Henry, please, this is ridiculous. I can't perform miracles. It's not going to work and besides, you'll be completely blind afterwards because I'll have to replace your eyeballs with his. Is that what you want?"

"I want my eyesight back. I don't care about nothing else. If it doesn't work, I'll take care of things, but you're going to try. And remember, if you think of calling the police or anything else, my neighbour has a video of you handing out drugs to schoolkids. If he doesn't hear from me in forty-eight hours, he'll go to the police." This was a lie, but Tom didn't need to know that.

Tom tried to argue back, convince Henry to read any article on the Internet to validate his claim but Henry wasn't listening. He'd been suffering for far too long now to back down. Besides, the guy strapped down beside him was beginning to wake up.

"Better get on with it, Tom. Tell me what to do."

Tom sighed, opened his mouth to say something else, then stopped. "Ugh, damn you. Get on the other operating table, but don't say you weren't warned. Good luck, Henry."

***

When Henry woke up, he momentarily forgot where he was or what had been done to him. He tried to open his eyes and found they were stuck. An initial wave of panic stole over him as he made to rub them then touched the bandages covering the top half of his face. He breathed a sigh of relief as he recalled now why everything was dark and his eyes stung.

"Tom, are you there? Where are you?"

There was no answer and once again a flurry of anxiety threatened to overwhelm him. Had Tom abandoned him? Gotten scared at the last minute and ran? He tried to sit up but a bolt of stabbing pain shot into the side of his head.

"Tom?" he called. louder. "Where are you?"

Still no answer and Henry really was getting worried. He felt around and touched the cold metal table he was lying on. He was still on the operating table, then. He thought of trying to take the bandages off, desperate to see the results. If it had failed, as Tom had said it would, he would tell Tom to inject him with something that would kill him instantly and his torment would be over. But he prayed this wasn't going to happen.

"Henry, you're awake."

Tom. Thank God.

"Tom, I was getting worried. How did it go?"

"I told you how it was going to go, Henry. I did it anyway and you know have that other guy's eyes. But I'm warning you; when I take the bandages off, you are not going to get your vision back. But before you can open them, it will take a while—you're still under the effects of the anaesthetic."

"Just do it. I need to know. And where is the other guy, by the way?"

"In a self-induced coma until we decide what to do with him."

This was the least of Henry's problems. If the operation worked he'd deal with the guy same as he'd dealt with all the others. "Take the bandages off, Tom."

Henry jerked as Tom slowly began to peel off the bandages. Now that it had come to it he could hardly stand the tension, the waiting until his eyelids opened and he could confirm a success or not. Once the bandages were off, he had to fight to repress the urge to physically push up his eyelids.

"Don't, Henry, you'll cause yourself harm. Just be patient and wait. It will take some time. Why don't I put on the T.V. in the meantime to take your mind off things?"

Nothing was going to take his mind off things, but maybe the quiet drone of the television would send him to sleep for a little while longer; his head was starting to ache again.

Tom turned on the T.V. The news was on. As he listened the impatience and anxiety was slowly replaced by horror. A deep, stabbing knot of terror invaded his whole body. He moaned and mumbled incoherencies to himself, his brain jamming, causing spasms in his arms and legs and his head rolled from side to side. He heard Tom muttering expletives beside him as the full realization of what they had done came to them.

"The man kidnapped, Timothy Reynolds, was waiting for his brother on the corner of Depot Road at Bradwell's main industrial site, when witnesses said they saw a man bundle him into a white Ford Escort and drive off, apparently unconscious. The tragedy of the case is that Timothy is blind and would have been incapable of defending himself. Police are urging the kidnapper to…"

Henry heard no more from the reporter as he screamed in eternal darkness.

Petri-Fried

Stuart Holland

This, to be fair, has not been the best week of my young life. Actually, I don't think it would be an understatement to say it has been the worst. I could begin by telling you just how badly it started off, but I won't. Suffice it to say I am all that is left of the former me and all that is left is one of my bright young eyes. Everything else of me has gone, I know not where. The fact is I am still here, even though I can't do much about my predicament. I've been cold, very cold, for the last couple of days, sat in some strange kind of liquid. Fortunately I have no sense of smell any more, that part of me disappeared along with the rest of my body a few days ago.

I am now sat in a round, clear plastic dish and am warming up nicely. The young woman took me out of the cold place a little while ago and the clear dish on which I am placed is on a wooden bench. I am looking away from the young woman to what appears to be some kind of demonstration taking place on a bench a few rows ahead of me. The person there is dressed in a white coat and is animatedly talking to the people in front of her. At least I think she is talking but I lost my ears as well as everything else a few days ago.

The demonstration must be over as the person in the white oat is walking in front of her bench.

Now, suddenly I feel something touching the outside of my eyeball. Whatever it is covers my pupil, leaving me in the dark. And then,..

"Ow, take a bit of care, that hurts," I try to say but my vocal cords have gone. Actually, it really hurts, or it would do if my brain hadn't also gone several days ago. Now I am left to my fate. I am handled and turned round just quickly enough to see another young woman, sitting next to the one who is holding me, faint. There is commotion, She is sat back up and escorted away from me, presumably out of the room. The person holding me stabs me again, harder. I know not what I have done to deserve thus, but she is not the nice person I thought she was when she took me out of the cold place.

"Ow, ow, ow," I try again. Something is cutting into me, snip, snip, snip, cutting away at the iris, exposing the lens of my eye. And then everything goes dark, but not the pain. I vow revenge on this young woman as I feel the lens of my eye pop out of the incision she has made. There is a pause; surely she is going to put it back together again?

Oh No! She has other plans. Suddenly I feel heat, real heat. The flame comes close to what is left of me, making the eye juice bubble and boil. Without warning, I explode, my juice spurting up into the young woman's face, burning her tender flesh. As I finally die I thank the pig-God that revenge has been served and I can now rest in eternity.

Tapetum Lucidum

David Turnbull

"Spooky, isn't it?" said Kate from the other side of the hotel room.

John sat in the bed, back propped up by the pillows, fired by their love making, enthralled by the green, almost phosphorescent glow that was strangely emanating from her eyes.

"Tapedum Lucidum," she said. "A layer of tissue behind the retina. It's usually found in certain type of animals. But round these parts a lot of people have it. It's genetic."

John chuckled nervously. "You're not a vampire then."

"No, John, I'm not a vampire. But I might just eat you."

She came slinking across the room, hips swaying, red hair cascading over her shoulders, green eyes glowing in eerie intensity. His pulse quickened in almost instant arousal. "I'm going to call you Foxy," he said.

She stood naked at the foot of the bed, smiling demurely, pale complexion freckled intensely from head to toe. "On account of my red hair and my sparkling eyes?"

"That," agreed John. "And the fact that you're so damn sexy."

There was a raw, musky smell about her that caused the blood to rage in his veins and roar in his ears. She lowered herself to the bed, crawled toward him, straddled him and nibbled his neck. "I'm going to show you what a naughty little vixen I can be," she purred as her eyes flashed luminously.

John exhaled a long slow breath as she ground seductively down on him.

***

John was part of a dying breed: A sales rep for a confectionary and soft drinks wholesaler, the friendly face who offered a personal touch to the proprietors of independent corner shops and convenience stores. But he could see the writing writ large on the wall. It didn't bode well. The advent of online sales and telemarketing, combined with big retail multiples driving his core clientele of to the wall, meant his choice of career was rapidly developing into a disaster.

Given this line of work, Government policies such as the sugar tax and anti-obesity measures were probably going to be the final nail in the coffin. Commission wasn't half what it used to be. He reckoned he had two or three years' maximum before the wholesale confectionary market would slump so badly he'd be forced to call it quits. Hardly enough time to build up a decent pension pot or any sort of financial cushion.

He wasn't even sure his knees would hold out that long.

Restructuring meant he now had responsibility for an entire region, not just a district. He was clocking up a shocking number of miles and spending way too much time in motorway traffic jams. All that time gunning the pedals was playing havoc with his joints and probably hurtling him toward early onset arthritis.

It was fatigue that persuaded him to pull off the motorway slip road and look for a hotel. Claiming overnight expenses wasn't as easy as it once was; they no longer went through on the nod. You had to provide receipts and your claim had to be signed by an accounts supervisor and countersigned by a regional manager before being forwarded to payroll.

On this occasion John felt so weary he didn't mind paying out of his own pocket and forgoing the bureaucratic process, just so long as he could collapse onto a soft bed and drift into sleep.

The Reynard was the first place he came across. It sat on the outskirts of a traditional looking village, set back from the main road. A tarmac carpark to one side. A little beer garden and children's play area to the other. A traditional wooden sign depicting a monocled fox in top hat and tails.

More of a pub with rooms to let than a hotel.

The bar doubled as the reception desk.

From the moment Kate checked him in and handed over his key, she'd started outrageously flirting with him. "Room seven," she said, glancing at the fob. "I'll have to keep that in mind." She pushed a lock of red hair behind her ear and grinned mischievously. Green eyes not exactly glowing at that point but glinting slightly, freckles speckling her pointed little nose.

John didn't know what to say or how to react. He was in his mid-forties and wasn't the type to go leering after young ladies. She had to be twenty years his junior. Sensing his awkward befuddlement, she changed the subject. "Are you hungry? I could get you a menu if you'd like to eat."

John looked at the name badge pinned to her blouse. "Kate, is it?" She nodded. "I may eat later. I've been driving since the early hours of this morning. I'm pretty beat. What I'd really like is to have a shower."

"OK, go freshen up and when you come back down just sit at that table by the fireplace and I'll fetch the menu."

"It's a deal." He picked up his key from the bar.

As he headed for the stairs she called after him. "Hey, John, if you need me to come and scrub your back, just pick up you phone and press zero."

She laughed as if it was a joke.

Is it just me, thought John, *or is she really coming on strong?*

***

He had thought of taking a nap after his shower, but it revived him a little and stirred his appetite. So he went back down to the bar and sat at the table by the fireplace as she'd told him.

A moment or so later she came sauntering across with a laminated menu. She'd tied her red hair back. Now that she was out from behind the bar he saw she was wearing a short black skirt, quite high above the knee. Her legs were lithe and pale, as freckled as the bridge of her nose. John thought she might have tantalizingly popped an extra button on her short-sleeved blouse.

She winked at him. "What took you so long, John? I've been missing you."

He tried to join in with the gentle banter. "I had to look my best for you."

"And you scrub up very nicely indeed," she said, laying the menu on the table. John looked down at it. She rested her hand on the table, tips of her red lacquered fingernails touching the skin on the back of his hand. A little jolt of excitement ran through him.

"I'd recommend the seafood platter with sweet chili dip," she said. "Quite the aphrodisiac, so they say."

Inside his shirt John felt a film of perspiration forming on his chest send a warm trickle running down to his belly. "I'll take that then," he said, voice almost catching on the pulse that thrummed in his throat.

***

Back in his room, he found he couldn't settle.

When Kate brought his food, her thigh had pressed so firmly against his upper arm he was convinced it couldn't be accidental. He kept going over and over it in his head. Was she just toying with him? If he went down to the bar right now and offered to buy her a drink would she laugh in his face? *No thank you, old man, you're old enough to be my father.*

He was about to fire up his laptop and email through the orders he'd taken that afternoon when there came a gentle knock on the door.

It was Kate.

She'd changed out of her work clothes into a light blue summer dress, patterned with a sunflower motif. Her hair was resting on her bare shoulders. John thought she was probably the most beautiful woman he'd ever seen.

"Just finished my shift," she said. "The manager asked me to pop up and see if there was anything you needed.' She bit her lip and stared into his eyes. That pulse seized his throat again. "Anything you need, John? Anything at all?"

"I don't think so" he said, regretting the words as soon as they tumbled out of his mouth.

She grinned mischievously as if she didn't believe it.

"Are you sure, John? Nothing you need?"

John was flummoxed.

What to say?

What to say?

"Well, there's the TV." It was the first thing that popped into his head. "I can't seem to figure out the channels."

"Oh, that's easily be fixed."

He moved aside and as she entered the room he was engulfed in her enticing musky smell. "Shut the door, John. You don't want any midgies flying in. There's much better ways to be kept awake all night than having a midgie buzzing at your head."

108

John did as she asked.

She picked up the remote control and stood facing the TV.

He waited a foot or so behind her, enthralled by the way the blue floral dress clung to the curve of her hips. As if sensing she was being watched she turned to face him. "Are you sure you want to watch TV? There are less boring things you could be doing."

That was a come on, thought John. *It was definitely a come on.*

What do you see in me, he wanted to ask. *What the hell could a beautiful young girl like you see in a stressed out sales rep with a middle aged paunch?*

Kate dropped the remote control to the floor and began to unbutton her dress.

"For God's sake, John, you're so slow. Just kiss me, would you?"

And so her steady seduction of him picked up pace.

In the years before his disastrous marriage and the years after his acrimonious divorce he'd had his share of one night stands but he'd never been seduced before. Never before swirled into such a rapid and deep intensity of passion, over which it seemed had no control whatsoever.

***

And now here he was with her head resting on his chest, heart still pounding from their third bout of love making, her eyes flashing like fireflies each time she blinked. He ran his finger through her hair.

Pinch me, he thought. *Pinch me, and I'll snap out of this dream.*

His eyelids were growing heavy. He could feel sleep slowly reeling him in but he was suddenly jolted back to wakefulness by a hideous high-pitched scream from somewhere outside the window. He felt himself tense. "What the Hell was that?"

Kate squeezed his ribs with her arm. "Relax, honey, it's just one of my cousins."

John turned to her. Her eyes gleamed greenly back him.

"One of your cousins?"

"A fox," she breathed. "You said you were going to call me Foxy. Foxes scream to communicate with each other. Probably calling out to its mate."

"It's a scary noise."

"I don't find it scary," she said. "We're used to it round here. I find it comforting. Like a song from back home."

"Where *is* home?"

"Not far," she replied, vaguely.

She stroked her nails seductively across his chest. "Get a little sleep, John. It's a long time to go before dawn and I'm not finished with you yet. Not by a long shot."

John didn't know if he could manage another bout. Her love making was hard and vigorous and physical. His back and hips ached. His groin felt numb. He had several appointments in the morning. He thought he might have to cancel them. He didn't think he'd be in any state, physically or mentally, to clock up more miles.

His eyes began to droop again.

Outside the window the fox screamed hideously.

This time it didn't prevent sleep from seizing him.

**

He awoke and found Kate's side of the bed empty. He waited a moment to see if he'd hear the flush of the toilet and see her appear in the bathroom doorway, eyes glowing, stepping nakedly toward him. The room was silent. The night was silent. No more foxes screaming beneath the window.

Had she left? Realised with sudden crashing clarity what a hugely stupid mistake she'd made? Picked up her dress and tiptoed away, ashamed, embarrassed - repulsed even? He was far from any sort of catch. She could do way better than him. Someone closer to her own age.

He reached over and switched on the bedside lamp. There was still a dull, throbbing ache in his back and hips. She'd really taken it out of him. He wished he'd met her when he too was in his twenties. Or even his thirties. Now he was just too out of shape. Too depleted of stamina.

When he turned around, he saw that she'd left him a note on *The Reynard's* headed paper, propped up on her pillow. He unfolded it, expecting some sort of apologetic rejection. *I'm sorry. I don't know what got into me.*

Instead, it was the exact opposite.

"Hey, sleepy head, have you even done it outdoors? Beneath the moon and the stars? Come find me and you'll get a big reward. XXX."

John read it again just to make sure he wasn't misunderstanding.

That little voice of insecurity whispered in his head again.

What the hell does she see in you?

He wondered if he should content himself with relishing the experience so far. Quit while he was ahead, as the saying went. It was 3am. If he slept till six, he'd get three hours in. Then he could sneak down, leave his key on the bar and simply drive away. Kate would think he was a complete bastard but she was young. She'd get over it. It wasn't as if he'd gone out of his way to pursue her. She was the one who'd made all the running.

He read the note again.

The answer to her question was no. He'd never had sex outdoors. He wondered what that would be like. How it might feel out there the darkness and the cool night air. He thought about Kate and the erotic way she moved against his body and he knew that if he didn't go, he would be cursed to wonder for the rest of his days. Wonder what it might have been like, out there beneath the moon and the stars.

Decision made, he took and quick shower and rushed his clothes back on.

Then he went downstairs and out into the night.

***

He saw Kate immediately. She was waiting for him on the other side of the road, standing still and silent. Her dress rippled a little around her thighs in the night breeze. Her green eyes gleamed, reflecting the light from the moon. John stood silent too, breath in his chest held tight in aroused expectation.

Kate turned and began to walk slowly away. Taking that as his cue, John crossed the road. His pulse thrummed in his ear. The breeze was warm and not unpleasant. It washed over him like a gentle caress. He felt almost as if he was sleep walking, seized by some sort of hypnotic influence, still somewhat incredulous that all of this was actually happening to him.

Kate kept looking back over her shoulder. He'd see a quick spark of green from her eyes, then she'd turn her head and walk on, almost as if she was making sure he didn't lose sight of her. He considered catching up with her, taking her hand in his and walking at her side. But he didn't think it was what she wanted. This *lead and follow* was all part of the seduction game she seemed to relish so intensely.

She led him along a dirt path and into a little wooded area. It had rained a lot during May and early June and the vegetation each side of the path was waist high and vividly vibrant. Serpentine fronds of fern vying for dominance amongst tall, bowing nettles and fat goldenrods.

The path was smooth and well-trodden. The air filled with the fertile scents of the soil and the abundant plant life. The boughs of the trees hung heavy with leaves, spread wide to maximum span. Every now and then he'd catch a glimpse of the moon. He felt suddenly imbued with a mystical almost primordial sense of oneness with nature. He wondered if this is how ancient man might have felt, walking a path such as this on a night such as this.

Kate came to a halt in a clearing, waiting for him. Green eyes glowed like neon beacons in the dark. *This is it,* he thought. *This is where it's going to happen.* His heart thumped in his chest, in his wrists, at the back of his neck, in his groin.

He stepped tremulously into the clearing.

"Take me from behind, John. Lift up my dress and take me from behind."

She turned and leaned the palms of her hands against the gnarly bark of a fat oak, bending her back slightly. Hands shaking, John unbuckled his belt, pulled down his zipper and did as she bade him.

And it was all that he'd imagined it would be, there beneath the stars and the moon, with the night breeze whispering around their tryst and Kate pushing forcefully back against his thrust. When he was spent he expected she'd turn around and they'd hug. Instead, she dodged him and wriggled free when he tried to embrace her.

He stood there, confused, breathing heavily from his exertions.

Then he saw what was there beyond the trees. Two sets of green eyes, just like Kate's, glowing and staring intently. Two men of similar age to Kate

114

stepped into the clearing. They weren't overly tall, or particularly muscular but there was a menacing arrogance in their swaggering countenance.

John instinctively moved in front of Kate.

She chuckled. "Are you trying to protect me? There's no need. These are my cousins, John."

Now that he looked closer, he could see the family resemblance. Not just the way their green eyes glowed, but the shock of red hair, the noses that were slightly pointed and abundantly freckled.

"This is Dan and this is Joel."

Somehow, he wasn't reassured.

The boys scowled back at him.

"If this is an ambush," he said. "Some sort of convoluted attempt at a mugging, you should know that my wallet, watch and car keys are all back at the hotel, locked in my room."

From behind him he heard Kate laugh again. "You think I don't have a pass key, John? We'll go and retrieve all of those things afterwards.'

John didn't like the sound of that.

"Afterwards?"

Kate stepped out from behind him and stood in the middle of her spritely cousins.

"After you've served your purpose."

You knew this was too good to be true, said the voice in his head.

"And what's my purpose?" he demanded, feeling righteously belligerent.

Kate grinned and rubbed her belly through the sunflower dress, green eyes seeming to glint with a deeper intensity. "To impregnate me. To give me the litter I long for. A brace of cubs to suckle. I've

115

tried before. Many times. Many men, just like you. But their seed has never taken. This time, John, I'm full of optimism. Literally brimming with fecundity."

John took a step back, appalled by what he was hearing.

"Who are you people?"

Kate carried on grinning. "I told you that Tapedum Lucidum is a common trait round these parts. That's only half the story, John. Centuries ago, the foxes in this area acquired a supernatural ability to transform into human form. We are their descendants."

That was preposterous. Did she think he was stupid? He might have fallen for her manipulative guiles, but he wasn't that gullible. If the whole situation hadn't unsettled him so much, he'd have laughed out loud.

"Look, if you're members of a pagan cult, or something and I've unwittingly gotten myself drawn into one of your fertility rituals, it's fine. Each to his own. Who am I to judge? I can get in my car right now and drive away. I won't look back. I won't ever come back here. I won't tell a soul about any of this. After all, as you said, I've served my purpose."

"I actually said *after* you've served your purpose," correct Kate. "You're almost done, John. But not quite."

From the direction of the village came a blood curdling cacophony of fervent, high pitched screams. Kate cocked her head and looked at him with her eerily glowing eyes. *Christ,* thought John. *I can see the fox in her. I can actually see it.*

"You hear that, John? It's beautiful. Like a midnight choir. The ladies are screaming on the lawn and it's all for you."

John an icy tingle frosting his nerve ends.

"All for me? What's all for me?"

"They're hungry for you, my poor depleted lover," said Kate. "Famished. Ravenous. They'll tear you to pieces and fight over your bones."

The terrible screams rent at John's ears again. To either side of Kate the red-haired cousins, Dan and Joel, stretched their pale, slender necks and screamed a howling rejoinder.

John fled.

***

He was disoriented. No idea where he was running to. No real clue as to how to get back to the hotel. Terrified, in any case, to go back that way, it was so close to the village. They might be waiting for him. Those ravenous vulpine ladies who apparently wanted to tear him to pieces.

He kept away from the path, hoping he might eventually stumble onto the road leading back to the motorway. He hurtled headlong through the darkness. Low lying branches scratched his face. Nettles stung his hands. Bramble thorns clawed at his trousers. Little spiky twigs penetrated the soles of his shoes, puncturing the soft flesh of his feet, drawing pin pricks of blood.

Every time he thought he'd reached the edge of the wood a pair of glimmering eyes would appear, glaring in menacing green luminosity, forcing him to turn back. In sheer panic he trampled through a twisting, interwoven colony of ground level ivy, catching his foot, falling forward and cracking his knee painfully on a rock.

He picked himself up and limped on, drenched in sweat, lungs fit to burst, knee bleeding profusely through the torn fabric of his trousers. He was unfit and overweight. Kate had thoroughly drained him of what little energy reserves he might have had.

He found himself back in the clearing. All he'd achieved for all his efforts was a chaotic and frustratingly torturous circle. A sharp stitch stabbed at his side. Exhausted he fell to all fours, agonising pain jolting through him from his wounded knee.

He became aware of Kate's long freckled legs walking toward him across the grassy sedge. "Give it up, John," she said, standing over him. "You can't outrun us. We know every inch of these woods. They're our back yard. We frolicked naked here as children."

Strong hands took a firm grip on his upper arms and he was hauled roughly back to his feet, Dan to one side of him, Joel to the other, green eyes glinting. Dan screamed. Joel followed. From the village the women screamed back. John vomited and wet himself.

They dragged him back along the path, Kate behind him. Every now and then she'd slam the open palm of her hand hard against his back to push him along. The expectant screams filled his ears and filled his head.

When they reached *The Reynard* he saw that each side of the road that led to the village was lined with red haired men and boys of all ages. Their green eyes glowed. They swayed as he was dragged past, in a horribly silent flowing rhythm.

John struggled and yelled and tried in vain to wrest himself free.

"Let me go," he pleaded. "Please let me go."

Kate's hand slammed into his back again, making him stumble forward. Dan and Joel held him upright. The screaming rose to a fevered crescendo. Up ahead was the village lawn. Dozens upon dozens of green eyes stared back at him, hellishly glowing with Tapedum Lucidum.

A pale, freckled hand shot out of the darkness and raked the flesh of his cheek with viciously sharp fingernails. He felt his face shred. Hot blood drenched his shirt. The screaming became frenetic and chaotic.

Dan and Joel let him drop. Kate kicked him for good measure.

The ladies of the village fell on him; biting and clawing and tearing.

Firelight

Leslie Gulvas

The creak of the crooked wooden door was lost behind the woman's morning song. Sunlight snuck into the cool gloom. When sunlight touched it, wool stuffed in the loose frame released a musty smell, as did the dark packed earth of the floor.

The woman's song smiled, acknowledging sunlight's arrival.

The curve of the red, rough adobe walls reflected sunlight around the stark room. The beams of the roof made a pattern of octagonal shadows. Clothes, then hanks of wool, then hanging herbs slowly emerged from the rafters. However, the mud stuffed hole in the center of the room, where the tin chimney fled from the cast iron stove, hid in the darkness of the roof, preferring anonymity.

The morning song danced joyfully around the room.

The woman's blind eyes weren't aware of sunlight's presence. Her skin acknowledged its warmth. Soon, the fire in the stove would add a challenging light to the round room. Sunlight could ignore that intrusion. It and the old woman had this morning ritual for ninety years. No mere firelight could compete with what they shared.

The morning song raised in pitch as the old woman opened the stove to add more wood. The wood wheezed with the heat and its sap popped, spraying the woman's dress with hot drops.

Smoke billowed out of the stove sunlight and made it sparkle to warn the woman, but blind eyes did not see. She waved the smoke away with an arthritic hand, stopping the morning song in a cough. More wood went into the fire. Another glob of burning sap jumped on the skirt. The stove's gaping mouth closed. The morning song continued winding around the room touching everything. The woman's hand reached for the coffee sack to continue her daily ritual.

Sunlight watched, alarmed as the glow of fire blossomed on the old woman's skirt. Sunlight had no control of fire's choices. A breeze entered the room, pushing back the smoke and feeding the tiny flames on the skirt. The skirt shifted as the woman stood. Her sightless eyes recorded none of the warnings of the objects around her. The skirt tried to resist the flames, but the rich lanolin and spilled drops of food in its weave welcomed the fire that consumed them.

The breeze fed the flames and the old woman's hair shifted and joined the fire. Hands beat at the skirt and the flames added them to the joy of leaping light. The morning song became a scream that wailed around the room, echoing the alarm of the other objects. Fire had tried to escape the stove for years and now it was free. The cloth and herbs hanging from the ceiling were next to join the fire's joyful dance.

No more octagonal shadows from the roof beams. They made light of their own as fire claimed them as fuel. The mud stuffed around the chimney cracked away against the battering flames. Fire called to the breeze which ran through the room and out the hole by the chimney. The door hosted flames where ashes of wool failed in their duty to stop the wind through the cracks.

Smoke, the fire's friend, pushed back the sunlight that was trying to illuminate the old woman on the floor. Her sightless eyes wide, melting, her blackened hands curled to her chest as tendons dried out with the fire's heat. Smoke pushed sunlight out the door.

A beam and its long-time compatriots fell, no longer capable as their ends turned to ash. The old woman's skull stretching with the pressure of boiling tissue, smashed as the beam gave up its job of holding the roof and crashed down.

Fire was ecstatic. It leaped from object to object, consuming all before it. The breeze chased the fire, feeding it air and watching it leap with joy. When sunlight retreated into the night, firelight danced and twisted among the ash and ruins.

When all that would burn was gone the short-sighted flames faded and gasped to their death. For a time smoke drifted around with the ash looking for the old woman to feed the fire that spawned it. All smoke found was ash.

The dawn sunlight gazed down on the blackened adobe. There was no morning song to dance off the walls. Gray ash gave off a bitter smell at sunlight's touch. The breeze stirred by sun light's warmth moved the ash which danced and swirled reminiscent of the fire that formed it. Ash settled when the breeze moved elsewhere. Sunlight caressed the bones that had once been the old woman.

The bones warmed at sunlight's touch; fire was gone and couldn't bother them again.

Vanilla Goblin

Rickey Rivers Jr

1.

I usually go walking to clear my head and today
Eddy wanted ice cream. So I could kill two birds
with one stone. There's something special about ice
cream in Autumn. A day like today was Goldilocks
weather. Everything was nice. Not too hot, not too
cold, but just right, a just right kind of a day for
walking.

To get to the ice cream shop I had to go through
the park downtown, the scenic route. The park was
a nice quiet place to walk through. There were paths
that branched out, some met and led to sidewalks.
Others intersected.

The grass was freshly cut and the trees were
well managed. One tree in particular stood out. It
was the big oak tree in the center of the park. You
could see it from the highway. It stood wide and tall
where four walkways met. Eddy and I had to pass it
on the way to the shop. Around the base of the tree
was a small white fence. Red, yellow and brown
leaves littered the pathway.

I thought of the past, a nice beach walk alone,
then not alone as a young man came into view.
Waves were crashing nearby and I could almost
taste the salt in the air. My bare feet slapped across
the cool sand and the moon shone bright and soft

124

overhead. The young man stood near then closer. He was my lover. At the time I didn't know.

Eddy brought me back.

"You see that, Momma?"

I didn't see anything. I told him no. Eddy said he saw something in the big oak tree.

"What did you see?" I asked.

Eddy said a pixie or a fairy or something peaking from behind the leaves.

"Wow," I said. "That's rare."

It's fun to play pretend. A pixie in the park, a fairy in the park, sounded like a novel. I laughed. And Eddy was looking at me. I saw him but paid him no mind. He's a kid. My thoughts didn't matter much.

Soon I was back to him. This time the young man spoke.

"The moon compliments you. You're so beautiful."

I still remember his voice. It was smooth, a movie star voice. Like he spoke in rehearsed lines, but I couldn't stop myself from hearing the script.

"I want to lie here with you, just on this beach and treat you like you should be treated."

Again Eddy went on talking. "You see that, Momma?"

I took my mind off the man and back to Eddy. "No," I said, "what is it?"

"I saw a goblin in the big tree."

I smiled. Children are wonderful things. We came to the intersection with the wide oak tree and I looked up, no goblin, no fairies, or pixies. In a way I was disappointed. Sometimes you want fiction, prefer it even. I watched Eddy circle the tree over and over and even try to climb it until he was tired. Then it was time for ice cream.

2.

Eddy was enthusiastic in the ice cream shop. He ran in and pushed the door backwards for me.

"Thanks," I said. "What a gentleman."

I sat down in the booth. Eddy looked over the wall at the ice cream varieties.

A wave crashed in my head. Soon I was back on the beach. His lips were on mine and his arms were wrapped around me. I sank in the booth with an elsewhere mind, the moon shone bright from a coast in the past. I was happy.

Then Eddy called me. "Momma!"

He was next to me, looking at me with those big wide eyes.

I was annoyed, but I only said "yes?"

"The man said what flavor do you want? I'm getting strawberry!"

"The man?" I said.

I looked toward the counter, expecting to see the man I wanted to see. Instead there stood a man in white with a matching cap holding an ice cream scooper. He smiled the kind of hurry up smile I understood.

"A single vanilla cone," I said. I'd said that before. I liked chocolate, cherry, but most of all I liked vanilla. It's a safe flavor, but it's reliable. You can't be disappointed. The young man had the same question back then. Except he said it like "What you want?"

And I said my choice and he said "Vanilla for Vivian"

And that made me smile.

He ordered my cone like "Viv say she wants vanilla."

I smiled and put my head on his shoulder, but he wasn't there.

Soon enough Eddy came back with two different cones.

"Ice cream for me, ice cream for you!"

He sat across from me and handled me a cone. He licked his first. I thanked him and stared at the lonely scoop. It was perfectly placed atop the cone, round and white.

"Don't you wanna it?"

I heard that, but it was Eddy. He had a bit of strawberry ice cream touching his nose. I motioned for him to wipe it off and he giggled. He knew the signal. Boys like to play in their food. Eddy wiped his nose and said, "we should take some to Daddy!"

And I didn't say anything.

"Daddy likes ice cream too!"

I said no. It would melt and it would.

"We can cover it up," said Eddy, "and rush it back."

"No," I said. No is enough, it should be enough, but it's never enough for Eddy.

***

I focused on the ice cream, still round and un-licked. A full scoop, full like the moon, it glared back at me. No cares from a scoop of ice cream.

"What's wrong?" he said, but he wasn't there.

The young man said the same thing Eddy said now.

"Momma, what's wrong?"

But I didn't say anything. I was thinking and it's rude to interrupt a person's thoughts.

"There's ice cream that's green like a goblin," said Eddy.

And I heard him say that, but he was saying things that only a child cared about, silly and useless things like goblins in trees.

"Momma, I want sprinkles. I wanna be like a pixie!"

That was fine. "Go get some sprinkles."

And Eddy left the booth and went to the man at the counter. The man smiled and went to the toppings machine. He seemed happy to be there, happy to do his job. The place was empty. He must have been bored.

Goblins and pixies came to mind and then there was the beach again. The mind of a parent had to lean toward reality, the beach, the young man, the kiss; all of it real but distant, in a way a kind of dream. My phone rang. Eddy was back at the table now. He was quiet, licking his ice cream.

I answered the phone. It was Walter.

"Hi, honey," he said.

"Is that daddy?" said Eddy.

I nodded. Eddy was like me, more excited to see the person who wasn't there.

"Hi, Daddy!" Eddy waved like his father could see him.

I told Walter Eddy said Hi, or I told Eddy Walter said hi. One of those happened, it doesn't matter. Walter called to check up on us. He said that much, but none of his words meant anything. I wasn't there. I tasted my scoop of vanilla moon. The beach walk was so vivid that I half expected to taste the ocean in return. But no, the ice cream was vanilla, boring vanilla and boring Walter.

The young man said the same without the Walter.

"A safe bet flavor."

I agreed, but I didn't care. I liked vanilla. It was familiar. It wasn't wild like mint and caramel, the young man's choice.

"I like the mix, feels good in my mouth."

Then Walter said "Alright, honey. See you at home."

Apparently he was still talking about nothing important. I hung up without a bye, a bye meant nothing if love wasn't there.

"What did Daddy want?" said Eddy.

And I said "Nothing, checking in."

But that wasn't true. He said something, must have been something. It just wasn't important enough to discuss with Eddy. Eddy, our son, it wasn't important enough to remember. Now I was alone again. The young man was gone. And I was on the beach near the shoreline. The sand shifted beneath me. I tried my best to keep steady. My feet sank with every step. It was hard to walk on the beach in my head. To walk straight was a troubling thing. If only the young man was there. He could hold me. He could love me, and do it right.

3.

"Momma, don't drop your ice cream."

Eddy's voice shouldn't be on the beach. It wasn't. The moon was overhead like it should be. So why was he talking?

"Look at that."

"It dropped."

"It's cool, Viv. We'll get you another."

And I was saying no because it was alright. I was just happy he came back.

"Don't leave me again."

"I have to," he said.

But that wasn't true and I said so too and the young man said, "I'll see you again, don't worry."

But I never saw the young man again and the beach was nothing anymore, nothing but a foolish girl thinking she could be with a stranger, a foolish desire to be with another with a husband at home and a child on the way. Nothing but nothing and that's what I was. It took me so long to see that.

And Eddy was looking at me across the beach, across the booth, staring right in my face. This boy was mine, all I had, all I could want. So why wasn't I happy? He was diving into his strawberry ice cream with sprinkles. He was happy, full of life, chewing and smacking loud and smiling at me, then he was coughing, then he was choking. His eyes went bigger than ever.

130

The foolish girl on the beach dropped her ice cream and the young man offered to buy her another, but the girl refused. She just wanted to be there with him in that moment. Not at some ice cream shop in a booth with her son, a husband waiting for them to come home. She wanted the real of the beach. And Eddy was gagging and looking at me and I was hoping he'd gag himself to the floor.

Watching Us Scream
and Beg and Die

Jim Dyar

I was there when the world ended and, like the other damn fools, we should have known it was coming.

The sky over the city was just as blue as it had always been. Soft fuzzy clouds drifted across the warm summer scene. Traffic rolled by outside the park where picnickers picnicked, vendors vended and bustlers bustled. I remember the sun—the warmth. What happened next ended my belief in anything good.

It was my daughter who spotted it first, guileless in the face of the absurd. Her gaze studied a cloud above her family. As she stared, it blinked.

"Mummy!" she called excitedly. "The clouds!"

Her mother, more harried than relaxed over the day's outing, turned to our child.

"What, honey?" she snapped. "It's a cloud. There's no need to get excited over it. There are lots of clouds."

Looking chastised but determined, the little girl tugged at my sleeve next.

"Daddy, it blinked!"

My wife gave up with a sigh, knowing it wasn't going away unless she looked for herself. She set the picnic plate down and followed my gaze upward.

The cloud had two holes straight through to the other side. They blinked once more. Not with some lazy, slow wind current that rolled the nimbus around to emulate life, but the quick motions of a living breathing being.

"Hmmm, must be some weird current up there," I managed as I stared.

Another pair of eyeholes blinked on another cloud. We watched for a moment, bemused.

My wife agreed as she picked up her plate. As she went to eat, an insane pressure slammed everyone to the ground. Trees splintered with force; windows shattered buildings broke. Followed on the heels of that came a sound, drowning out the painful screaming with something beyond the noise. It didn't bother with banging around and echoing off things. It settled in our heads.

As personal as death.

We who were the ones who were lying down who survived. The people on their feet were crushed, bones splintering as they screamed out in agony.

People in vehicles hit unseen walls with no give and no care. Through death, they managed to escape what was coming.

TAP

Some fought to rise, to run. To get away from the crushing force that didn't give a damn that physics didn't work that way.

TAP

Trapped in terror, all of us remaining alive could only lay and absorb the third round.

TAP

133

Then sirens were coming from hopelessly far away for people who honestly didn't know how hopeless those forlorn noises were. I was carried from the scene, unable to manage more than a whimper in pain. My wife had been kneeling; my daughter had been standing. Of all the people that had surrounded me, I was one of the few that was scraped up and carted away. The last view of my family was two bloody smears as the ambulance door closed.

***

In those hours after the attack, rumors swirled, terror gibbered and those who believed they lead vowed to find "those responsible." Finely meticulous people went over every minuscule piece. Theories were advanced, people assigned blame and, strangely, nothing appeared to be resolved despite the bustle. My ragged body lay watching the television in the emergency waiting room. Every scene burned into my brain as people grasped at straws to explain the madness in such a way the world would suddenly become sane.

How could it? A mere three hours later, the terror hit again, a mere 8280 kilometers away.

***

I was still lying in a bed stranded in the waiting room, swaddled in a warmed blanket to ward off the shock. Unable to cope, my trauma-fuzzed brain idly wondered how many people would die before I'd end up being treated.

Amid my dark thoughts, the picture jolted and I stared.

"We are taking you now to a live feed from 58 news," the commentator exclaimed as the screen swung jarringly.

I stared.

The camera angle pointed upward on a busy street. I didn't recognize the buildings on either side. But it was someplace far more metropolitan than where I lived. I stared in horror. I could tell what was coming next.

What I recognized were the clouds.

No mere nimbus, they had changed. More face-like, but with some casual ambivalence and the hints of beards could be seen. The most significant change was their eyes.

Something had happened since the park. These were no mere cloud patterns but had manifested irises and pupils. From those clouded faces came an awareness. I stared in horror.

The buildings began to crumble from the top. Some whole buildings managed not to be crushed but were instead driven into the ground. With shock, I realized they were being shoved into the underground as if mere concrete and iron meant nothing.

Screaming came over the mike as the building collapsed reached the ground.

The camera fell as its holder succumbed. Screams turned to gurgles.

Then I heard it again.

TAP...
TAP...
TAP...

***

I must have passed out because it was dark when I came awake. Hospital or not, the lights had gone out.

I tried to rise although wrapped in my blankets,. One leg didn't work right but fortunately wasn't broken. Not so much for my ribs as I made my way off the pallet and over to a window. Outside in the dark, snow spiraled. Inside it was just as cold. My sinews cried out their own protest in tune with my groans as I tried to make my way through the emergency room doors.

Inside the chamber was nothing frozen bodies and rubble. A huge shaft of ice had pierced the roof—far too much damage to be merely a collapsed roof.

How had I missed all of this? The noise must have been incredible. I took a pair of crutches sticking out from a badly damaged closet and tried to make my way back out the front doors.

The snow swirled around me as I made my way out into the world beyond.

***

The cold is ever-present, food is scarce and survivors all have this haunted look, myself included.

136

We hide in the underground and huddle where we can. We bolt like rats and try not to stay in the same place for too long. We cower in fear and that's the only role left to us. Our pride, our hubris, our damnation and we cannot even shed tears.

All it takes is looking up to know why. There were no clouds up there, only faces. The faces of gods lured to our world by our constant inhumanity to our fellow man.

They were tapping on the glass of the world that holds us as they gaze into our hearts and find them lacking.

Cold Offering

Colin Leonard

My father's eyesight had gotten so bad that he couldn't legally drive anymore. He could still make his way around the neighborhood, squinting and prodding as if part of some cruel treasure hunt, but there was no way he could get behind a wheel. He tried not to let it bring him down. He enthused over the audiobooks I downloaded for him. He still roared at the football on the television if I came round to watch a match but I think he was following the undulations of crowd noise rather than the blurry lumps of colour shifting around on the screen.

"Get them checked regularly," he'd say to me. "The eyes. That's the one thing I wish I'd paid more attention to."

He'd follow that up with a quick subject changer. He didn't want to wallow in his afflictions.

The driving was a loss for him. He had thoughtful neighbours who helped with the groceries and I squeezed in visits between work and trying to have a social life but it meant his independence was truncated. I tried to make sure I was available if he needed a lift outside of town, for the big things at least, like… for his cousin's funeral.

His cousin McCabe passed away when a deluge of diseases finally persuaded him that ninety years

138

was long enough to have hung around on this earth. That branch of the family had deposited themselves in an unattractive patch of the Midlands many decades before and had just the right amount of dour humour to fit in as if they had sprouted from it.

My satnav fulfilled its promise to steer us there on time but that was still too late to get a parking spot in the church grounds. We tucked the car in behind a line of others at the base of the hill on which the church's broad body was mounted and we trudged up the road. It was a relatively modern building; solid black roof and chunky architecture gave it the look of an agricultural building decked out in armour to repel outsiders.

We dipped fingers in the font and wet the sign of the cross on our heads. A crinkle of motion from the front, the shapes of half-remembered relatives.

"Sit near the back," whispered my father. "I don't want to be hobbling up there like some old man with a stick."

I swallowed my smart-arsed answer before it came out. He could be sensitive about getting old. We settled into a pew but didn't dare remove our coats. There was a coldness in the church that infiltrated the heaviest of clothes and picked out the most sensitive joints, chilling calves and ankles, contracting the bones around the knees.

The only time I went to church anymore was for weddings and funerals but all the rituals were still inlaid deep in my memory, the mutter of responses, the elegance of the hymns, the bowed heads. It had been a long time since I had visited this part of the country but the place seemed strangely familiar.

"I've been to this church before, haven't I?" I asked my father under cover of a wave of mumbling prayer.

"Back when you were a child. Do you remember it? Your great-uncle's funeral. My uncle."

"Vaguely. What age was I?"

We sat back as those giving the readings were invited forward.

"I dunno, young, maybe nine. There was a big scene."

The first reader came to the microphone. A Reading from The Book of Wisdom.

"The souls of the righteous are in the hand of God," she began.

She had a familiarity of features common to all in the front two rows, must be a McCabe, probably a second cousin of mine. Would I even recognize that connection if I met her in the outside world? It was so long since I had seen any of these people. Years of experience on their faces patched over the faded tracks of childhood and disguised them as much as my flaky memory. A second woman spoke, a Reading from the Prophet Isaiah. They might have been sisters. Both readings were delivered with defiant, almost angry voices, challenged by the wind that blustered against the windows.

I could remember the church alright, but why had I made a scene back then? I recognised this church and its people in the same way that I thought of this locality; a tough, humourless place weighed

140

down by hard work and no distractions. Other than a slight progression of fashion in their clothes, it could have been the same congregation as when I was a kid. Practical, joyless haircuts on the women. Stoic noses red from the weather. People here held life as something to be endured and mistrusted. Their church wasn't a place that offered solace as much as resolve.

The mass ended. We joined the procession of those paying respects to the immediate family. My father shuffled up beside the coffin, straining his poor eyes to root out some recognition of the frail body within. I recalled something from all those years ago in the polished russet of the coffin's wood. Approaching it as a child, my heart hammering with fearful curiosity. A trepidatious chin peeping over the silk-lined edge.

We lowered our heads, moved our lips as we shook the hands of the bereaved. Some of them knew who we were, acknowledged by the patted hand, the sighs at what the years had taken from my father. After all condolences had been given, the funeral director closed the coffin lid and a phalanx of male relatives rose to offer their sturdy shoulders.

"Was I afraid of seeing the body in the coffin when I was a boy?" I asked under my breath. There was an image impressed on my mind, like a faded watermark, of an unnatural, waxy face.

"Something scared you. I had to carry you screaming out of the church."

Colourless, tight lips. A fear that the eyelids might open. But there had been more, it wasn't just an old man's dead face that had turned my nervousness into a frenzy.

We stepped out through the oppressive archway and just then it felt as if somebody clasped me across my shoulders and the back of my neck. The sensation was like heavy wings had dropped down on me from above. I twisted around, expecting to see a tall man towering over me with big hands and a hearty chuckle of how he remembered my face, but there was nobody there. Well, there were lots of people there but nobody close enough to have clapped me on the back like that apart from an old couple curled over their rosary beads. My skin itched beneath my jacket and it felt heavy and sodden. The strange discomfort shocked me but it was familiar too, like an old injury had been aggravated. A massage with claws designed to create panic rather than relaxation.

Rain wept from clouds the shape and colour of smudged mascara. I didn't want to stay out in it for long. I didn't want my father to get drenched and risk catching flu.

"We should go," I said to him.

"We have to stay." He positioned himself among the corridor of bodies formed to allow the coffin to be carried through and lead us to the graveyard at the side of the church.

"You'll get sick."

"We have to stay for the burial."

The priest passed by our bowed heads. The coffin bearers followed. I relived the angst of the young boy I was when first inside that church. The sides of my neck tingled. I remembered a voice, offering to do something, a cold menace to it.

Sunday shoes crunched on gravel. The tail of the cortège invited us to join it. I gripped my father's arm and extricated him from the slow swarm of mourners.

"Stay back here against the church wall for a bit of shelter," I implored him. "I don't want you to be next into the ground."

We pressed our backs against the building and only our faces suffered the swirling spit of rain. I squirmed my shoulders against the stone, trying to release the feeling that something had clenched onto them. A tight muscle maybe, a spasm, a rash.

Heads and heavy coats sloped up towards the grave, blocking our view, disembodying the solemn tones of the priest. The amplification of a portable PA system curdled his words to a drone that those of us on the outskirts could follow only by inflection. Eventually, the sounds settled to a finality. Rainfall filled the silence before a stir of motion and mutterings enveloped the crowd. Small pockets of people edged towards the hole in the ground and the chief mourners.

"Come on," I said. I wanted to get away from this miserable place. "It's too wet to go up there. How many times do we have to tell them we're sorry for their loss?"

He allowed me to lead him away without too much grumbling.

We weren't the only ones not hardy enough to deliver graveside condolences. I recognised an aunt and her decrepit husband among the early escapees.

"Are you going up to the house?" she asked after we caught up to them, their snail's pace even more hampered than ours.

"Aye," said my father and shucked a nod in my direction. "We should be staying here shaking hands, by rights. This lad is off-colour, I think."

"We'll all catch our deaths in this weather," my aunt replied. "There'll be plenty of time to talk to everyone at the house. You don't look all that great yourself."

The three of them tightened in a collusion of health complaints. I trudged on towards the car, hunched against the cold. I yanked up my collar but a chill still pierced my ear, a wet breath waiting to speak. I didn't like churches. As soon as I hit my teenage years, I had refused to go to mass anymore. I wondered if it was a memory from this dismal place that put me off, as much as trying to stake a claim of youthful independence. Being manhandled out of there, a quivering, squawking child; that had to have an effect. Why had I gotten into such a state? I knew that I didn't want to see the deceased but I just had to stare in at him, like a boy with a stick is impelled to turn over a dead bird. I had to look but I didn't want to see. A voice in my ear. Cold, chill. A pressure around my shoulders. Had it been my father? Was it the priest? No, the priest had been at the altar. I could picture him framed there. The adults were all squeezing each other's hands, dabbing tears. I had ferreted through a tunnel of sombre suits, drawn to the corpse in the box, trembling to investigate then shuddering at the sight.

144

A freezing cold hiss in my ear - *Do you want me to cover your eyes?*

It definitely hadn't been my father's voice.

"Jaysus, wait for me, will you?" That was my father's voice. He was abandoned behind me, the apprehensive tap of his stick in one hand, the support of a parked car under the other.

"Sorry, sorry," I trotted back to gather him. "Where are the others?"

"They're in their car. You just kept walking on without me. I couldn't see you properly. Which car is ours?"

"Sorry, I got lost in my head. I was trying to remember that funeral when I was a boy. That one is ours." I guided him back by two cars and opened the passenger door.

"You walked past it? Thought I was the blind one."

"Yeah," I lent an arm to assist him into his seat then got behind the wheel. "Dad, did I say anything at the time about why I got so upset?"

My shoulders and neck slumped forward, as if under a wet, icy towel. Perhaps taking my jacket off would relieve the pressure. It didn't. I started the engine and indicated to pull out.

"I feel odd," I said.

"I don't remember if you said anything. It was so long ago. You took a bit of a fit. You were pulling at your face, I remember that, and rubbing your eyes."

Do you want me to cover your eyes?

145

Clammy movement around my neck. Wet and soft like a hand with slugs for fingers. The cars in front lined up to take a right turn at a junction.

"I don't feel good at all. Do we have to go up to this house?"

"It'll look bad if we don't go. They'll have soup and sandwiches. You can have a cup of tea if you're not feeling well."

I pulled at my collar and grated my shoulder blades against the car seat. My foot slipped from the clutch and the car cut out.

"What's the matter?" said my father.

"It feels like there's something on me."

I started the engine again and crept up to the turn. The windscreen wipers complained about their worn blades with a persistent squeak.

"Something on you?"

"Something stuck on my back. Since leaving the church. I feel shivery. It feels like something has latched onto me."

"Are we at the first turn after the church yet? You need to take a right here," he said, floating a hand in that direction.

"I know. I'm following all the other cars."

"It's a dangerous turn, this. You need to be careful pulling out."

Our breaths polluted the glass. I turned the heater up full to fight the condensation and counter the raw, cold clamouring around my neck and my ears.

Do you want me to cover your eyes?

"I remember there was a voice," I said. "Lisping, ghostly, right inside my ear, a mean, nasty voice."

Cars coming from both sides.

"The body in the coffin, your uncle, that freaked me out but I couldn't look away. Then there was a voice from behind me."

Do you want me to cover your eyes?

"I said yes to it. Yes, I said. Cover my eyes. Then the fingers slid round. It was like ice slipped in under my eyelids and I couldn't see and I started screaming and I tried to pull it away, to get it off me."

It was hard to judge the distance of oncoming vehicles in the rain. The car behind me gave an encouraging beep.

Do you want me to cover your eyes?

"Same voice now, Dad. You don't hear it, do you? You can't see it on my back, can you? I think it clung onto me again back in the church, just as we left. It must have remembered me."

My pupils grew cold. I took my foot off the brake.

"I don't want it to cover my eyes, Dad. I don't want to be blind."

A Fresh Pair of Eyes

Dona Fox

<u>Susan</u>

Initially the eyes were like the new tennis shoes I got every summer, the ones that felt as if gravity had forgotten my name. These eyes cracked every color so hard I wanted to cry. I didn't remember the world looking so beautiful.

I pushed the quilt back real slow so as not to wake Nick sleeping in the bed beside me, tiptoed to the bathroom and shut the door. Call me a narcissist but it had been so long since I'd seen myself. I slipped my nightgown to the floor, savoring the sight of each imperfect inch of my skin until I heard movement – Nick packing in the bedroom. I knew this was coming.

"That's it, don't tell me otherwise, I know you can see just fine now, Susan. Connie's been a real trooper through this—it's time for me to go home." He buckled the plaid suitcase, grabbed his toothbrush and went into the bathroom. The last thing I ever saw clearly was his fine ass. Truly. That's when my left eye went totally dark and my right went gray.

"What's wrong with you?"

"Nothing, just go."

***

148

Callie

I woke with a start. Initially I thought the weight that landed beside my head was the cat so I reached over to pet her and gently guide her off my pillow but instead of soft fur I felt a bulge–rough, and damp.

"What the hell?" I stretched my other hand behind me, worried for my husband. And with good cause; he wasn't there. I scooted across his side and off the bed. "Allan?" I whispered as I reached to turn on the lamp.

The lamp wasn't there.

Allan must be in the bathroom. I rushed on the familiar path; I ran into a wall.

Now my nose was bleeding. I had been trained to sterile techniques until they were second nature; so I couldn't touch my nose. But the blood was dripping on my feet, running onto the floor, creating a hazard. Allan might run back into the room unsuspecting, slide and fall.

I'd use my pillow case to staunch the flow, but now I couldn't find the damn bed. Finally, I removed my pajama top, tore off one sleeve and held it against my nose.

I slipped the one-armed pajama back on.

I felt for a light switch. Nothing.

Cautiously I crossed the room, searching for something familiar, I found the bed but not one other piece of furniture. Besides the bed; the room was empty. I knelt and felt the floor. Unvarnished planks. No carpet. This wasn't my bedroom. Was I in the middle of a nightmare? Could I scream my way out? I'd done it before.

I stayed next to the wall and circled the room looking for a door or a window from which to escape. If there were any, they were carefully hidden.

I returned to the bed. I sat down, the mattress sagged and something rolled next to me and hit my hip. This time I picked it up.

It felt like a wet gunny sack. The contents were warm and loose. Should I open it?

The bag was yanked from my hands.

"What's it feel like to be alone in the dark?" The voice was that of a young woman.

"What do you want? Where's my husband?"

"One question at a time, please. Do you remember me by the sound of my voice?"

My mind swept through a thousand possibilities; friends, relatives, chance acquaintances, employees-past and present, patients-past and present. Of course, I must have had unhappy co-workers and employees from the past and in the present; didn't everyone to one degree or another? The same went for patients–that's what insurance was for, no one was perfect though God knows I tried and I wept alone when I failed.

Which brought me back to reality. I had a full schedule of surgeries today. Patients that had waited months, hoping for the so-called miracles that I might be able to deliver. Sure, I'm not irreplaceable but all the other surgeons were booked up months in advance also. Some of my older patients might not be around to enjoy the new sight that I could have given them.

"Obviously you don't. What if I told you my name? Susan Eddie. Do you remember me now? Tell me something about myself. Who am I? How did we meet? Where did we meet? What were your last words to me?"

So not a relative, then. "Listen, Susan. I have to get to work. A lot of people are counting on me. Please, tell me what you want. I don't have much time but I'll try to help you if I can."

She giggled, then she laughed and then she was coughing, choking. And she turned on a spotlight that shone on her face.

Both of her eyes had been gouged out. The sockets were scarred and dry.

"You already helped me. You did this."

"No. I didn't do that, Susan. No. Never."

"Your colleague, we'll call him Dr. B, did some surgeries on my left eye and my vision was just a little bit fuzzy. You were to make it clear. I wore an eyepatch for weeks. I was so hopeful. When I took it off, I couldn't see anything at all. You said, it may take some time for your vision to come back. Six weeks later you said, 'I'm so sorry, I scraped off too much, there's nothing to grow back.' And that was that. Goodbye. I never saw you again. Gradually I realized what having one eye meant. In a fit of anger, I gouged them both out. So you did this."

"What do you want from me? Money?"

"No."

"What then?"

"I have these two special eyes I'd like you to glue into my sockets." She held out two hazel eyes and a monster glue stick from the hardware store. I wasn't going to debate the physiology with her.

"Where did you get those?"

She giggled, "Allan. I also have the eyes from the cops he called, just in case his don't work." The wet gunny sack landed in my lap. "And lots of your neighbors."

I was sick, "If you've already killed my husband why should I do anything you ask?"

"Allan's fine. He's in the basement. Come on, give me the cop's eyes. Hurry up and I'll leave."

"You'll need a painkiller."

"Not for glue. Do you think I'm stupid? This is purely cosmetic."

"Okay. Give me the glue. Hold one eyeball in each hand and tip your head back, give one to me when I say ready."

She tipped her head back and her mouth fell open. I rammed the glue stick as far down her throat as I could–cap still on so the glue wouldn't cause any permanent damage, then I found her phone and called an ambulance for her.

Using her light, I found the basement. Allan was tied down there and thankfully he still had both eyes. I untied him and took the gag out of his mouth. I used Susan's phone again to call a cab.

In the cab with Allan, I called my Chief. I told him everything that had happened and said I had to come in, my surgeries needed to go ahead. Brusquely, he put me on hold.

When he came back on the line he said, "I know you think I'm a blundering old man but I've kept my hand in for a reason. I review every upcoming surgery so that I'm ready, just in case, and Callie, don't worry, I'm ready."

I broke down in tears, "I don't remember this woman."

"That's because she wasn't your patient."

"Even so, that could have happened to me," I was relieved, but not enough to throw another surgeon under the bus.

"But it didn't happen to you; wouldn't have. Come back to work tomorrow. This place, your patients, need you too much. Think about it overnight."

"Okay, I will." And I knew I'd go back tomorrow, because that's what I did, that was my life.

Then our cab pulled up in front of our house. My body, tense for so long finally relaxed. We were home.

As the cab pulled away, I noticed how quiet our community was, then doors slammed up and down the lane. Allan and I turned to face the neighborhood and saw our friends and neighbors as they streamed down the street toward us. It was only as they drew closer and surrounded us that we realized they had no eyes; only empty, bloody sockets where their eyeballs should have been.

Meet the Authors

Dan Allen is Canadian and enjoys spending time in Northern Ontario. You can find his short stories in numerous magazines, anthologies and podcasts. Visit www.danallenhorror.com to see a presentation of his published work.

His terrifying look at Alzheimer's, "Above the Ceiling," is featured in Bards and Sages collection of the Best Indie Speculative Fiction Vol. 2.

A personal favourite, "Sympathy for the Zingara," can be found in the March 2019 edition of ParAbnormal Magazine.

His terrifying story, "The Basement" (edited by Horror Zine's Jeani Rector), was published by Hellbound Books in July 2020.

You can visit Dan at www.danallenhorror.com and follow him on Facebook and Twitter at @danallenhorror. You can write to Dan at contact@danallenhorror.com

Olivia Arieti lives in Torre del Lago Puccini, Italy, with her family. She writes drama, poetry and fiction. Her stories have appeared in several magazines and anthologies including, *Enchanted Conversations, Enchanted Tales Literary Magazine, Fantasia Divinity Magazine, Forgotten Tomb Press, Horrified Press, Infective Ink, Pandemonium Press, Sirens Call Publications, Blood Song Books, Black Hare Press, Pussy Magic Magazine, Stormy Island Publishing, Breaking Rules Publishing, Scarlet Leaf Review, Iron Faerie Publishing, Dark Dossier*

Magazine, Paramour Ink Press, Raven and Drake Publishing.

Justin Boote is an Englishman living in Barcelona and has been writing for five years. In this time, he has published around forty short stories in diverse magazines and anthologies, including ten for Scare Street's Night Terror series, a novelette called Badass with Terror Tract Publishing, two short story collections on Amazon called Love Wanes, Fear is Forever, Volumes 1 and 2, and numerous short stories.

He has also written a trilogy to be published in the summer and is currently finishing a five-book series, while also outlining another.

He can be found at his Facebook author page https://www.facebook.com/BooteJustin

Rie Sheridan Rose multitasks. A lot. Her short stories appear in numerous anthologies, including Killing It Softly Vol. 1 and 2, Hides the Dark Tower, Dark Divinations, and On Fire. She has authored twelve novels, six poetry chapbooks, and lyrics for dozens of songs. She is also editor-in-chief for Mocha Memoirs Press and editor for the Thirteen O' Clock imprint of Horrified Press. She tweets as @RieSheridanRose.

Dona Fox writes short stories and poetry - horror and dark fantasy, infused with bits of science fiction. Coming from the Pacific Northwest, specters from the damp evergreen forests, Portland's bridges & Seattle's streets, often creep into her dark tales. Her stories are generally told by slightly mad narrators, full of sadness, who find themselves in dangerous situations where the edge of reality is always in question.

Dona's story *Walking on Water* appears in the Bram Stoker nominated anthology, The Beauty of Death vol. 2: Death by Water, published by Independent Legions, edited by Alessandro Manzetti.

She has two collections of short stories, Dark Tales from the Den and Darker Tales from the Den, both published by James Ward Kirk Publishing. Also, she has appeared in various anthologies published by James Ward Kirk and J Ellington Ashton Press publications in the United States and Horrified Press publications in the United Kingdom—and she appears in the original issue of *Cemetery Dance Magazine*.

Find out what Dona's reading and sign up for her newsletter online at www.donafox.com

Audible: https://www.audible.com/author/Dona-Fox

Amazon Author Page: https://www.amazon.com/author/donafox

Goodreads: https://www.goodreads.com/author/show/7352292. Dona_Fox

Leslie Gulvas is a collector of experiences, a retired science teacher and a former research scientist. She lives on a little farm with a giant wolfhound and a disgruntled guard pig. Her writing features average people in extraordinary situations. Writing as Skeeter Enright, she has an urban fantasy novel, CARNIVAL CHARLATAN, and a Native American thriller OFF THE RESERVATION written as Lee Gull. Under her own name, she has over twenty published creative nonfiction articles and a children's picture book IGGY THE CONFUSED PIGGY. Her websites are: https://leegull.weebly.com and https://skeeterenright.weebly.com

Colin Leonard lives in rural Co. Meath, Ireland, beneath the hills from which the ancient Samhain festivals spawned Halloween. His stories have been published in the magazines *Dark Tales*, *Frost Zone Zine*, *Fudoki*, and *The Harrow*. His flash fiction appears in anthologies from Black Hare Press, Breaking Rules Publishing and Ghost Orchid Press.

Wendy Lynn Newton is an Australian fiction and non-fiction writer. She is the author of two non-fiction books and her short stories and feature articles have appeared in many key international and Australian literary and media publications. Wendy is a Full Member of the Australian Society of Authors and spent several years as a member of Write Response, a team of independent Tasmanian arts reviewers, after being selected by Arts Tasmania for an arts@work mentorship. She is currently working on a young adult science fiction trilogy and lives in northern Tasmania with two out-of-control Chihuahuas and two indifferent cats.

wendy.newton.launceston@gmail.com
Instagram: @wendynewtonlaunceston

Rickey Rivers Jr was born and raised in Alabama. He is a Best of the Net nominated writer and cancer survivor. His work has appeared in the JJ Outre Review, Stellium Literary Magazine, Fabula Argentea (among other publications).

Liam A Spinage is a former philosophy student, former archaeology educator and former police clerk who spends most of his spare time on the beach gazing up at the sky and across the sea while his imagination runs riot.

David Turnbull is a member of the Clockhouse London group of genre writers. He writes mainly short fiction and has had numerous short stories published in magazines and anthologies. His stories have previously been featured at Liars League London events and read at other live events such as Solstice Shorts and Virtual Futures. He was born in Scotland, but now lives in the Catford area of London. He can be found at www.tumsh.co.uk.

Stuart Holland is the owner of Fiction4All, a golf enthusiast (especially the 19th hole) and has written in the genres of crime/mystery, thrillers and suspense and has now turned his hand to horror. His books are available from fiction4all.com in both digital and print editions. His other interests include conspiracy theories, the Knights Templars and he has a fascination for the paranormal and supernatural.